IN THE HEART OF THE STORM . . .

Bang . . . crassshhh! Ricky stood where he was, heart pounding. The lightning was getting awfully close! King began to go crazy, barking and whining and scuffling his nails on the floor.

Smasssh . . . crassshhh! "That was right on top of us!" Ricky whispered. A loud, moaning wind had started up, and he could hear it swishing in the branches of the trees. Behind the cabin, the old white pines bent and groaned and heaved.

CRASSSHHHHHHHH! The last crash was so deafening and horrendous that Ricky didn't notice, at first, the splintering, crackling, sound that accompanied the big bang. When those sounds continued, terror filled him.

"That's not lightning!" he shrieked. "The trees . . . the pine behind the cabin . . ." The big white pine was falling! "Run, dog!" Ricky shouted. "The tree's coming down on top of us!"

Bestsellers from SIGNET VISTA

THE LAKE IS ON FIRE

MAUREEN CRANE WARTSKI

A SIGNET VISTA BOOK
NEW AMERICAN LIBRARY
TIMES MIRROR

PUBLISHED BY
THE NEW AMERICAN LIBRARY
OF CANADA LIMITED

WEST ISLAND COLLEGE

RL 4/IL 5+

Copyright © 1981 Maureen Crane Wartski

This is an authorized reprint of a hardcover edition published by The Westminster Press.

First Signet Printing, December, 1982

2 3 4 5 6 7 8 9

SIGNET VISTA TRADEMARK REG. U.S. PAT. OFF. AND FOREIGN COUNTRIES REGISTERED TRADEMARK—MARCA REGISTRADA
HECHO EN WINNIPEG, CANADA

SIGNET, SIGNET CLASSICS, MENTOR, PLUME, MERIDIAN and NAL BOOKS are published in Canada by The New American Library of Canada, Limited, Scarborough, Ontario
PRINTED IN CANADA
COVER PRINTED IN U.S.A.

Remembering Dad and Harrius

ACKNOWLEDGMENTS

I would like to express my thanks to Don Candlen of the Foxboro State Forest Service, to the members of the Sharon Fire Department, to Barbara Weinberg, to Rita Lapointe for sharing her expertise on dogs with me, to Mike Murray for telling me about the fisher, and to Mark Wartski for his painstaking assistance.

1

Ricky heard the dog barking. The sound crept into his dream and changed it, somehow. He had been dreaming that he and Leo were hang gliding together, laughing as they tested their skill and strength against the currents of the air.

"Hey, Rick!" Leo was shouting. "Look at me . . ."

Ricky came awake, still feeling the buoyancy of the wind, still looking at Leo. He opened his eyes and stared into darkness.

"*Look* at me, Ricky!" Ricky Talese closed his sightless eyes.

There was a specially made clock near his bed that would have told him the time, but Ricky didn't bother to reach for it. It was late in the afternoon. He knew that, because heat was pouring through his west-facing bedroom window. He wondered briefly if he should reach for his white cane and get up, then he rejected the thought.

"To heck with it!" he muttered.

The dog barked again. Ricky frowned. So he

hadn't dreamed that sound. What was a dog doing in the house? Mom had had a dog once, a fat dachshund, but it had died many years ago. Suddenly Ricky sat bolt upright on his bed.

"They haven't got a seeing-eye dog for me!" he cried. "I won't have it! They can take the damned dog back."

He heard his bedroom door open.

"Ricky, are you awake?" his mother asked.

Ricky didn't answer. He felt impatience and an aching longing to bury his head in his hands and burst into tears. His mother could see, couldn't she? She could see that he was sitting up in bed!

"There's a dog in the house," he accused.

"Not *in* the house. King's in Deirdre and Sol's Bronco. The dropped by to visit and they had to bring their new dog with them."

I'll bet they dropped in, Ricky thought wryly. He knew that his parents had invited the Gallaghers out of desperation. They had been pussyfooting around him for two weeks, ever since he had taken his white cane and tap-tapped his way into the bathroom, found a razor blade, and tried to cut his wrists.

"They wanted to see how you were getting on," his mother was saying in the timid, pleading voice he dreaded. "Won't you come down and say hello?"

"I'm kind of tired."

Once, Deirdre and Sol had been his favorite people, and he and his best friend Leo Kraemer had practically lived in the Gallaghers' cabin up in the White Mountains. He and Leo had gone fishing at Bobcat Lake and built birdhouses for Deirdre to hang in the tall white pine behind the remote cabin.

"I don't know whether I'll get up or not," Ricky said.

"Ricky, please. They just want to . . . to see you." Mom didn't say words like "look" or "see" too easily.

She was obviously going to stand there until he said he would come down.

"Okay," he said at last. "I'll be down in a bit."

He listened to the sound of his door shutting, then to the receding footsteps, and waited for the memories to come. He knew that they were crouched inside his brain waiting. Whether he was awake or asleep, the memories were more real than anything that had happened after the accident in February. He and Leo had gone skating with a bunch of guys, riding in the car Leo's big brother had borrowed from his dad. They had been laughing, talking about vacation, groaning about school, and teasing Leo because he was in love again. And then, there was the patch of ice, a skid, and the screaming and the crunch.

He could still hear that horrible crunch! The car had been squashed as it skidded into a tree beside the road. Of the car's six passengers, three had survived, though with severe injuries. Leo had been killed. Ricky had been blinded.

Ricky felt himself sweating as he remembered the rest. He would never forget how his parents had broken the bad news to him as he lay, all bandaged up, in his hospital bed. He would forever remember Dad's voice, sounding strained and torn, as it spoke about Leo and then added, "There's been a problem with your eyes, Rick. You must try and hang on, because this is tough news."

And then his mother had cried. It was Ricky's first real memory of his blindness—Dad's voice, and Mom crying, saying, "We're so lucky. Poor Leo. We have you still, Ricky. Thank God you're alive."

Ricky had been too stunned to thank anyone. Later, reality set in. When he left the hospital, the world was an unfamiliar place. Everything that had been his—his room, his stereo, even the bathroom shower—seemed unknown to him.

"You'll get used to it, hon," his mother said, encouraging as she guided him past the living-room coffee table. "Here's the couch, remember? I'll never move it, so you'll have a point of reference. And here's the kitchen, the refrigerator. It'll get easier."

Definitely easy if he could see. Perhaps easy if he had tried. But what was the point in trying? There was no hope of regaining his eyesight; the doctors had told him as much. No sense going back to school, either . . . and he hated his friends who could run on the track team and throw a basketball into a hoop and go to the movies. They pitied him. He could hear the pity in their voices when they came to visit him. The pity oozed through the little pep talks they gave him. Like: "Gee, Rick, it's too bad. We'll miss you on the track team. But you'll run again, man!" Or, "Ricky, don't give up. There are decent schools for the blind. They make good books in braille." And finally: "Ricky, just think of Helen Keller!"

He had shut his ears to the voices and the pity and the pep talks. He had locked himself in his room, where he lay listening to tapes he and Leo had made during their last vacation together, tapes mostly of the Beatles. He listened to the cadence of their voices and thought about dead Leo, and then about John Lennon, who had been shot and killed. Perhaps that was when he had started thinking about the razor blade in the bathroom as a way out.

"Rick-y!" His mother's voice interrupted the memories. "Ricky, are you coming down?"

He drew a deep breath and got off the bed, found his sneakers and fumbled with them, trying to distinguish left from right. Then he put the sneakers on and tapped his way to the door, opened it, and stood in the hall facing the stairs. As he slowly made his way down the stairs he heard the sound of welcoming voices rising toward him.

"There he is!" Sol Gallagher called. Sol wasn't a

5

very big man, but his voice rumbled and boomed out to enfold Ricky. "What's this? You've lost weight!"

"He doesn't eat much," Mom sighed.

Ricky frowned, exasperated. He hoped his mother wasn't going into her I-worry-about-him-so routine. He tried to walk down the stairs casually, but knowing that they were all watching him made him clumsier than usual. He tripped, lost his balance, and slid down the last three steps on his bottom. No one said anything, but he knew that they were all holding their breath. He knew Mom was looking at Dad, and that her eyes were full of tears.

"Oops," Deirdre Gallagher said, breaking the silence. "Are you okay, Rick?" He nodded, hoisted himself to his feet, struck out again with his white cane. "Come over here and sit beside me on the couch," Deirdre continued.

He barked his shin on the side of the coffee table before he found the couch. As he eased himself down on it, his father said, "Hungry, Son? Your mom made apple pie, your favorite."

"It's good pie," Sol put in. "Your mother's a fantastic cook. I thought you'd be as fat as a pig, Rick. All that lying around since February."

Ricky suddenly hated Sol. Did he think it was fun "lying around"?

"I think you're right, Sol," Dad was saying. "Ricky does need exercise."

"Sure!" Ricky snapped. "I'll go out and run four miles or so. All right? Or maybe I'll play basketball with the guys. Better still, why don't I get into my football gear? I need to keep in shape to play this September!"

There was a little uncomfortable silence, and then the dog barked again. Its barking held a deep, ominous note.

"That's only King," Deirdre told Ricky. "He's a German shepherd. Our new orphan."

"Not a very friendly orphan," Mom said. She put a plate on the coffee table in front of Ricky. The pie, Ricky supposed. He made no attempt to reach for the plate. Did his mother really think he'd eat with all of them watching? He could hardly stand the thought of eating when he was alone. It was disgusting how he had to struggle and slobber and mess with the food he couldn't see.

"Oh, well," Sol was saying, "they were going to put him down, you see. A fine animal like that! King's had a sad life, you know. His first owner had to move away when the dog was a year old, and the man who next bought him beat and starved him. Finally, King turned on the brute, and the man got frightened and decided to put King away."

"Except that you took him in," Ricky heard his dad say. "That's not surprising."

Ricky knew what his father meant. Deirdre and Sol were both social workers by profession, and noted for the way in which they took all hopeless cases, human or animal, under their wings.

"King eats like a garbage disposal," Deirdre said. "That's a good sign. At first he wouldn't eat . . . snapped at us, snapped his collar, too! I suggested we put a choke collar on him, but Sol wouldn't hear of it. So, we got an extra-strong collar for King, and a long leash, and we gave him lots of understanding and waited for him to snap out of it." She paused. "He's come a long way. He tolerates me, now, and he'll let Sol touch him. If anyone else looks at him crossways, though, his hackles go right up and he starts to growl."

"Suppose you can't tame him, Sol?" Ricky heard his father ask. "You'll have to put him down, won't you?"

"He'll be all right," Sol said. "We're taking him up to the mountains this weekend." There was just a tiny pause before he added, "How about you, Rick? Want to come?"

Ricky knew now that he had been set up. He knew it from the deliberately casual way in which Sol spoke. He could just imagine Mom on the phone to the Gallaghers: "Dee, Sol, I just don't know what to do anymore! You know how Ricky walked into the bathroom and slashed his wrists with the razor blade. Luckily he didn't know how, and he didn't bleed very much, but . . . it scared us so! He's been so changed since the accident. Leo's death . . . well, you know that Leo was like a brother to him! And we're afraid he might try to kill himself again. The psychiatrist at the hospital said that half the kids who attempt suicide try again."

"Well, Rick?" Dad asked. "That's an interesting proposition." Dad was part of the setup too, of course.

"The place misses you," Deirdre urged. "Bobcat Lake is so full of fish that even Sol managed to catch a mess of bass! They tasted super."

"We could walk the trails." Sol's deep voice lowered to a persuasive growl. "We could get away from some of this summer heat. Any more weather like this without rain and I'm going to wilt up and brown out." He paused. "I could use some help, Ricky. I'm aiming to cut down that big white pine behind the cabin, but Deirdre says no. You can help me convince her that the tree's half dead and might topple over if we ever get a good rainstorm."

"Sol's an alarmist," Deirdre argued. "There isn't a thing wrong with that tree. Come up to the cabin and tell him so, Ricky!"

Ricky listened to them. The loneliness that never quite left him boiled into a red-hot lance of pain. How could he go back to the Gallagher's cabin without Leo?

"It'll be good for you," his father was urging. "Go, just for a week or so! Think about it, Ricky."

"I don't want to . . ." but it was pretty hopeless.

The adults had all made up their minds, and if he tried to get out of it, they'd just work on him till he agreed to go.

"We're leaving in two days," Sol said. "You'll have a great time, Rick. I guarantee it."

Ricky thought of the White Mountains. He thought of Leo clowning and falling into Bobcat Lake. He thought of them both camping in a bed of poison ivy and itching for weeks. He thought of the long moonlit nights when they had talked about their plans of going to college, maybe becoming pilots someday. He felt like screaming and smashing things.

Outside, King started to howl. A week with Sol and Deirdre giving me pep talks and a bummed-out dog to keep me company, he thought. Great. Super. Terrific!

2

Ricky knew from the beginning that the trip was going to be a disaster. When he stepped out of the house that morning and heard Sol shout, "There you are! Hurry up, kid, the hills are waiting!" he had to stifle an impulse to retreat back into the house and hide.

Instead, he got into the Gallagher's Bronco. Sol insisted on Ricky's sitting up in front with him.

"King's tied up in back, but he's easier around Deirdre than he would be around you," he explained. "Sit up here, and we can talk."

Ricky hated the idea. There was nothing he wanted to do less than talk. He leaned back in the front seat while Sol rambled on and on about the fun they would have at Bobcat Lake. "Ricky, those fish are biting! I've got a new lure that no self-respecting bass will pass up."

Why didn't Sol just quit talking? Ricky wondered. Did he think he had to keep on with the zippity-do-dah bit? He wished Sol would just shut up, and maybe Deirdre read his mind, because a half hour into the long drive she said, "Sol, you talk too much."

Sol took the hint, and that was worse. Silence was always worse. Ricky caught himself remembering the last time he and Leo had gone up to the cabin with the Gallaghers. That was last October, just when the leaves were at their peak. The memory of all those colors—scarlet, red, crimson, yellow, and gold—made Ricky feel dizzy. At the time he and Leo had been too busy listening to a football game on the radio to care about colors. Who cared about a few old trees? There would always be time, later, to see a New England autumn.

"Would you like the radio turned on?" Deirdre asked.

That started Sol talking again. "Okay, Rick, what kind of sounds do you want? Pop? Rock 'n' roll? I don't know what you kids have instead of ears, always listening to that ear-splitting racket."

Ricky knew that Sol was baiting him, hoping that he would argue. In the old days, he and Leo and Sol had had some good, old-fashioned, knockdown arguments. "Why?" Ricky asked himself wearily. "What was so important that you had to argue about it?" He turned his face to the window, staring into his own personal darkness.

"We're still on 93," Deirdre said, mistaking his movement. "There's a long drive up ahead of us."

"I think I'll take a nap," Ricky said. It was easiest to retreat into sleep. He leaned back against the car seat and folded his hands over his stomach, over the tight clasp of his safety belt. If Leo had worn a safety belt that day, he thought, he might not have been killed. Then he wanted to weep with frustration. Why did he always have to remember the accident and Leo?

Ricky pretended to sleep for quite a while. Although he couldn't see where they were going, Deirdre and Sol kept him informed by talking to each other. Here they were turning off Route 93. Now they were on the Kancamagus Highway. Suddenly Deirdre sucked in her breath.

"What's the matter?" Ricky asked.

"Look at that! Oh . . . I didn't mean . . ." Deirdre hesitated, then added quickly, "There's been a fire here. The trees have all been burned and the underbrush and grass is charred. It looks like a war zone—complete desolation."

"It was just a small brush fire," Sol soothed. "It couldn't have happened too long ago, Dee. I didn't notice it the last time we came up here. Of course, this summer has been bone-dry. I'll bet there hasn't been an inch of rain in the last ten weeks."

"They've been hoping for rain for days," Deirdre said. "So far, all we get is bright, hot summer. The grass looks limp, Ricky. Even the trees seem tired."

Ricky did not reply. He was thinking of the word

Deirdre had used—desolation. He felt as if he were the burned-out area she had described. He murmured the word to himself, liking it.

"What did you say?" Sol asked. "Didn't hear you, Rick!"

Just then King started to bark. The dog had been silent till now, and his loud woofing startled Ricky.

"What's the matter with him?" he demanded irritably. "Does he have to get out, or what?"

"Maybe he's just tired of riding. I know I am," Sol said. "Pretty soon we'll come to the gorge, and we'll stop there and stretch our legs and let old King sniff around a bit."

When they came to a stop, all of them got out of the Bronco. Deirdre stayed with Rick while Sol walked the dog. They were not alone in the scenic rest area, Ricky knew. Several other motorists had paused to marvel at the gorge. The view, Ricky remembered, had been pretty awesome.

"I've never seen anything like this, never!" A woman with a Midwestern twang in her speech was talking close to them. "Are you folks from near here?" Deirdre replied that they had driven up from Massachusetts. "Why, you're next-door neighbors to all this beauty. Imagine being able to come here whenever you felt like it. I could just look and look. What about you, young man? Couldn't you just feast your eyes—" She stopped, fell silent.

Ricky didn't know whether he should just stand

there or turn away or get into the Bronco. He could feel the woman's pity.

"I'm so sorry," she said. "I had no idea! I'd never hurt anyone's feelings . . ."

Her voice drifted away, and Deirdre touched Ricky's shoulder. "Don't go getting thin-skinned on me, Rick. She didn't mean anything."

He shrugged irritably. Was it thin-skinned to mind when other people looked at you like some kind of alien? To hate pity and embarrassment?

"Where's Sol?" he demanded.

"Here he comes now. I thought we'd eat a bit of lunch . . . and then start on again." Ricky said nothing as Deirdre went on. "We'll be at the covered bridge in just a while, and then we'll be off into the mountains. We brought a lot of stuff with us, so that's why we didn't need to stop in Lincoln today."

Lincoln was the small town nearest the mountain cabin. Ricky was grateful that the Gallaghers hadn't stopped in town. He had been spared the gawkings of the Lincoln townspeople, many of whom knew him, had known Leo.

Deirdre set out lunch, but Ricky wasn't hungry. They ate, then drove on again, turning off from the Kancamagus to cross the covered bridge Ricky remembered so well. When they were well past the bridge and jolting up Blackberry Road, the dirt road that led up the mountainside, Ricky did drop off to sleep.

He was awakened by Sol's shouting, "Well, here we are!"

Where? Ricky wondered. Confused and disoriented, he sat up. He had forgotten that he was in the Bronco, but King's loud barks reoriented him.

"Had a good nap?" Deirdre asked. "You snored all the way up Blackberry Road. Scared all the squirrels and the birds away with your noise, too."

Ricky couldn't even pretend to laugh. Now that they were at the mountain cabin, he knew that he should show some enthusiasm, but the plain fact was that he was sorry he had come. He didn't even want to open the door and get out. He sat where he was.

"Here, come and hold this!" Sol commanded.

Reluctantly Ricky got out of the Bronco, eased himself onto the ground. Then, feeling disoriented again, he quickly put out his hand to touch the Bronco and steady himself. As he did so, Sol put a smooth, leather leash into his hand.

"Hold King's leash for a minute, will you? I have to get the bags and stuff down for Dee. If I let him run around now, he might take off and get lost."

Ricky held on to the leash uncertainly. He wasn't quite sure how to react. It wasn't easy relating to a dog you couldn't see. King tugged at the leash, and Ricky tried tugging back. The unseen animal at the other end of the leash growled a deep warning.

"Hey," Ricky said aloud, "don't take it personally, dog! I don't much care if you take off down the mountain or not, but Sol wants me to hold you. Stay put!"

The dog moved again, tugging at the leash. This time, it took Ricky's entire strength to hold him where he was. Muscles he hadn't used for months bunched in his arm and shoulder.

"You two having a tug-of-war?" Sol demanded.

"Yeah, and I'm not doing too well," Ricky snapped. "Come and take this dumb mutt off my hands, Sol!"

"In a minute." Sol's voice was calm. "The sun's got a way to go before it sets, Rick. Sky's all red— it's going to be another hot, dry day tomorrow. Want to take a quick trip down to the lake before supper?"

"No." It came out abrupt, and he guessed he was sorry, but there was nothing he wanted to do less. "I'm tired," Ricky said. "I just want to rest, that's all."

There was a silence, and then he felt Sol's hand on his shoulder. "Sure, Rick. Whatever you want to do is okay."

Ricky handed the leash to Sol and turned away. The man understood how he was feeling, all right. In a confused way, Ricky wished that the Gallaghers didn't understand quite so much, didn't know him quite so well! He wished that Sol wouldn't talk about Leo.

"It's too bad about Leo," Sol said, deep voice gentle. "You two were like brothers. Planning to go to U-Mass together, and all. Planning to go to aviation school someday. Plotting to get hang-gliding lessons behind your mothers' backs." He shook Ricky gently. "He was a good kid."

Ricky stood silent. He tried clenching his hands, and found that his right first was clamped around the knob of his blind man's cane.

They went inside the cabin a short while later, Sol leading King and guiding Ricky, too. At the door of the cabin Sol left Ricky momentarily. He said he was tying King to the front-porch rail. "We'll bring his supper out to him. It's a fine evening, and I want him to snuff around and get used to the place."

The big dog whined softly. Was Sol actually patting the monster on the head? Ricky wondered. He, personally, wouldn't be caught dead putting his hand out to a big dog that growled so fiercely! But King made no protest as Sol patted him.

"Almost got so's you trust me, right?" Sol was saying softly. "You're going to make it, King. Ricky, you should see him. He's a beauty—big and tough, with a black-and-tan coat and big, smart eyes. The man who trained him to be mean should be horse-whipped!"

Inside the cabin, Dierdre had supper ready. "Cold chicken and potato salad," she announced. "I made plenty because you guys always eat like horses out here." But later, when Ricky had no appetite, she was upset. "Is *that* all you mean to put in your mouth, Ricky Talese? I've fed more to the birds!"

Sol told Deirdre to let Ricky be. "He'll find his appetite in a day or two," he said.

Ricky doubted it. Later that night, he lay awake in his bunk in the extra room where once he and Leo had talked till dawn. He listened to the sounds the mountain made. He could hear the creaking of the big white pines behind the cabin, and the sounds of insects in the hot, dry night. He heard the rustles of the underbrush that surrounded the cabin, and listened for the hoot of an owl and for the snarl of a faraway bobcat.

He lay with his eyes open . . . open, closed, what difference did it make, anyway? . . . and wondered how he could stand to be here for even another day. Memories pressed into his skull, making the loneliness inside him too heavy to bear.

At last, though, he fell asleep, and he slept late. He knew it was late because he could hear Deirdre's voice and King's deep woofing and the sounds of birds scolding and cheeping and caroling outside the cabin.

For just a waking second, he felt happy. I'm up at the cabin! he thought, and sat up on the bunk before he remembered he couldn't see.

He stayed where he was, not knowing what to do next. Should he lie back down? He wanted to.

Maybe he could sleep through an entire week. If he pretended he was sick or exhausted, he wouldn't have to do anything.

But before he could think this out, the door to his room creaked open and Sol rumbled, "Good grief, what are you doing, catching up on your beauty sleep? No use, man. With a mug like yours, you could sleep for fifty years and get no improvement in your looks."

"I was tired."

"And I'm tired out waiting for you! Get up and get dressed and have breakfast. We're going fishing!"

Ricky had to get up and struggle to put his clothes on right, fumble for his socks and sneakers. All the while, Sol hung around making dumb jokes. Ricky was guided to the bathroom and then to the kitchen, where Deirdre took over. She pushed him into a chair and set plates before him on the table.

"I'm not hungry," Ricky said.

"Mr. Talese, you are not getting up from that chair until I see you eat. I won't have you going back to your folks looking like a half-starved rat. Your bacon is at twelve o'clock, your toast at three o'clock, and your omelet is at nine o'clock. Do you want coffee? I'll pour it in a mug for you."

It was humiliating being told what to eat, where his food was! Ricky forced himself to eat, forced himself to listen to Sol map out their day. "Deirdre doesn't want to come with us. She says she's going to spend the whole day reading a good book and relaxing. So, we'll take a lunch and go down to the lake with the Bronco. It's a long walk."

But they had walked it, run it, so many times when Leo was there! Walked, and stuffed their cheeks with blueberries and blazed the trees for trails, and laughed and sung with happiness and excitement.

He pushed his plate away. "I'm really stuffed. Honest!"

"I've packed you a big lunch," Deirdre sighed. Ricky felt his hands being taken, felt something dry and crumbly being thrust into them. "For the ducks on the lake. Duck bread. Remember?"

Of course I remember, Ricky pleaded silently. Don't say anything more!

"You and Leo trained the ducks on Bobcat Lake. They come to us now, when we go down there. They're a greedy bunch."

He stuffed the bread into the pockets of his jeans. "I don't know if I want to go fishing," he began.

"The desire will grow on you." Sol grabbed Ricky by the arm and propelled him toward the door. "We'll be back before sunset, Dee."

There was no escape. As they left the cabin, Ricky stumbled, kicked into something soft and furry. A yelp and collision panicked him. He moved backward too quickly, fell, and was menaced by something huge and angry that stood beside him in the dark. He shrank from the snarling and the growling, and then Sol said, "King! Cut it out!"

King growled again, but Ricky could feel the big dog moving away. "You scared him by stepping on him while he slept," Sol explained. He helped Ricky to his feet. "You okay?"

"He's dangerous!" Ricky snapped. He found that his hands were shaking. He tried stuffing them into his pockets to hide the shake, but found his pockets jammed with duck bread. "He could've bitten my throat out!"

"Sure, he could have. He could have chomped off your arm or leg, too, for that matter. But he didn't!" Sol sounded pleased. "King's coming along. Aren't you, boy?" The dog whined softly as Sol led Ricky down the porch steps. "He didn't know you kicked him accidentally, you see. His former owner kicked him whenever the mood struck."

Ricky followed Sol to the Bronco, climbed in. He was made to hold the fishing rods while the rest of the tackle went into the back. Then Sol, talkative, cheerful Sol, got into the Bronco next to Ricky and started to talk up a storm.

And all the time I'm remembering, Ricky thought miserably. He could see it all so vividly, and in such detail. It hurt him to smell the pure, hot, fir-and-balsam air of the mountain and not see the tall spruce and pine trees, the hemlock, the birch, and the shy wild sarsaparilla with its funny, torn-looking leaves and bunched blue berries. His mind wandered over the whole east side of the mountain, past mountain yarrow, small daisies, everlasting; past inquisitive chipmunks and squirrels and beady-eyed raccoons. He thought of the cattails and the frogs by the lake. Had it changed at all?

"The lake hasn't changed, Rick," Sol said. "The trees still crowd around it, practically hang their branches into the water. It's beautiful and as untouched as when you last . . . were here." He paused a moment, added, "One of these days I guess other folks will use this bit of mountain and put cabins on it. I can't say I look forward to that day. I like the east side untouched—unchanged."

But it has changed, Ricky thought. He grit his teeth as the Bronco slowed and stopped. They were at the lake. "Sol . . . ," he began, but Sol was out of the Bronco and whistling through his teeth.

"Come on, Rick. The fish'll have given up on us by now," he called cheerily.

It was hot. Ricky was guided down to the lakeside where he sat down on the gritty sand. He dipped his fingers in the lukewarm water and thought he could feel shade from the beech and pine and spruce that ringed the lake. He smelled bayberry and pine. I should be glad that I'm here, but I hate it, Ricky thought.

Sol put a fishing rod in his hand. "It's all baited,

Rick. Just let 'er go," Sol said. "Want to put a side bet on as to who'll catch the most fish?"

The fish were plentiful. Ricky had to admit that. But the tug of a fish on his line, once so exciting, now made him sad. Leo and he had learned to fish up here one summer when they had visited the Gallaghers. They had wanted to have their first fish— little catfish—stuffed. Instead, Dierdre had found an old aquarium, and they had kept the fish all summer, let them go when they left the mountain in September. Suddenly Ricky lowered his rod.

"Heat too much for you?" Sol wanted to know. Ricky shook his head. "How about some lunch, then? There's nothing like food to pick you up when you're feeling tired. Or we could just talk—"

"No!" Ricky shouted. He was beginning to tremble all over. "I don't want to talk! I don't want anything! I just want you to let me be!"

There was silence. "I never wanted to come here," Ricky whispered. "It was my folks' idea, not mine. I just want—" he broke off, and felt the summer air pressing close with all its memories. He heard the zhee-zhee-zhee of a passing chickadee and the cheerful croak of a nearby frog. "I just want to be left alone," Ricky finished.

"Let's go back to the cabin." Sol reached out for him, but Ricky shrugged the hand away. "Rick, believe me, all we want is for you to be happy. We just want to help." Before Ricky could speak Sol added, "But you need to want to help yourself, too."

"Help myself do what? Learn braille? Tie my shoelaces like a good boy? Tap around with my dumb little cane?" Ricky was shouting again. "I'm tired!" he yelled. His voice echoed against the mountains. I'm tired . . . I'm tired . . . tired . . .

"It's hard, I know." But what did Sol know? What did anyone know? "It's been hard for you, Ricky. I know the memories are hard to live with. Take one day at a time." Now Sol put an arm around Ricky's shoulders. "We understand how it is—"

"You don't know what you're talking about!" Ricky pushed Sol's arm away and turned and started to fumble and grope his way back to the Bronco.

3

Ricky was grateful when they reached the cabin. It was hot, and the rasping of the cicadas made it seem even hotter. He wanted to be alone in the cool of the spare room, and even before Sol had parked, he jumped out of the Bronco and struck out on his own toward the cabin. He thought he could make it, but halfway up the path he tripped over a fallen branch and fell. Instantly King began to bark.

Deirdre came hurrying out. "Back already! Where's all the fish?" she exclaimed, then was silent.

"We didn't feel like staying, it's so hot," Sol said, behind Ricky.

"It sure is," Deirdre agreed quickly and much too cheerfully. "I was listening to the radio just now and it said that, if we don't have rain soon, the White Mountain National Forest will be into the worst drought they've had in ages."

Sol helped Ricky to his feet. "It's probably the heat that has us all jumpy."

Ricky didn't reply. He started to make his own way toward the cabin again, but when Deirdre came to help him up the porch steps he let her guide him inside. "You didn't even feed the ducks!" Deirdre said. Then quickly she added, "But you can always do that tomorrow. Maybe it'll be cooler tomorrow."

They're treating me like a sick person, Ricky thought. His head hurt.

"Are you hungry?" Deirdre was asking.

"No. No, I think I'll go and lie down." No one said anything. "I think I can find my way."

He left and tapped his way down the hall. The bunk bed felt cool and welcoming for a moment, then adjusted to the heat of his body. He lay with his eyes wide open, hands clasped behind his head. I really exploded at old Sol today, he thought. I shouldn't have done that. But why do they keep pestering me?

He knew why, of course. When he moved his head, he could feel his wrist rub against his cheek, could feel the lateral cuts that he had made with that razor blade. Why couldn't my folks have just let me go? he wondered miserably. It isn't as if I'll ever make it. Even if I ever learn braille, learn to get around without falling over everything, so what? The best I can hope for is to get some dinky little job in a place where they hire the handicapped. He thought of the things that he and Leo had planned to do. Hang gliding. Flying.

"I'd really be flying blind," he muttered, then laughed a short, bitter laugh. Now that he thought of it, there were so many expressions dealing with eyes. Blind driveway. Blind curve. Blind fear . . .

"I tell you, we should never have done this."

The words, faint but unmistakable, made him prop himself up on his elbow and listen. There was a mumble of meaningless words from Sol, and then Deirdre said, "It was a mistake."

They were talking about him, of course. Ricky got off the bunk and went to the wall of the room. He leaned his ear against the wall and heard Sol say, "What else could we have done? Linda and Andrew were going crazy. They didn't know what to do with the boy. We both thought it'd help him to come up here."

Deirdre sounded sad. "He's like a zombie. I look at him sitting. Sol, he never used to stand still! He and Leo were always into something." Her voice broke on the last word.

"He's like a bitter old man, fifteen going on eighty," Sol said. "At the lake today, he flared up at me. He thinks we're just watchdogs. He thinks that his folks set us up to guard him."

Deirdre sounded as if she were crying. Ricky felt a tightening of his insides. He remembered his mother crying at the hospital, telling him how lucky he was to be alive.

"Dee, give him a chance. He's hurt and baffled

and scared. Maybe we've been riding herd on him too closely. Maybe we need to give him space." Sol sounded thoughtful. "Maybe we should just leave him alone, let him do things on his own."

"He doesn't *want* to do anything!"

"All the same—" Sol's words were drowned out by King's loud barking. That damned dog, Ricky thought irritably. He was sick of King and his hostility. He could still recall his panic, that morning, when the mutt had knocked him down!

He went back to the bunk and lay there till he was called to eat supper. He could hardly choke down the food Deirdre piled on his plate, but no one said anything as he struggled to spoon the food into his mouth. Instead, Sol and Deirdre talked about the heat, about the ducks on the lake, about King— anything, Ricky thought wryly, to keep the conversation going.

After a while of this chatter Deirdre said, "I think we're going to have to drive into Lincoln tomorrow. We need a few things. In this heat the ice chest can't keep stuff fresh for too long."

"It'll be a long hot ride," Sol said. "Rick, what about it? You can come with us into Lincoln or stay here. It'll probably be cooler up here at the cabin."

So that was what Sol had meant by giving him "space"! Ricky nearly laughed at their simplicity. Did they really think he was so dumb that he wouldn't realize what they were up to? But the idea of being without Deirdre and Sol for a while was appealing.

"I'll think about it," he said. "I'll probably stay up here."

They let the subject drop. After supper, Sol and Deirdre cleaned up and then Sol got out his harmonica. When he heard the first familiar whine of the instrument, Ricky felt himself stiffen up. Sol always played the harmonica in the evenings, and when Leo and Ricky were around they had had concerts which, Deirdre swore, made the bobcats and coyotes head for the highlands.

"Want to sing a few tunes, Rick?" Sol now asked. "I'm pretty rusty, but you can't sing anyway. We make a fine pair."

Ricky said, "No thanks. I'll just go sit on the porch steps for a bit."

"All right. I've put King in the back, so you won't fall over him or anything. Just don't go far, Rick." As if he could.

Ricky fumbled his way to the door and stepped outside on the porch. The tremulous warble of the harmonica followed him as Sol played, "Oh! Susanna," "She'll Be Coming Round the Mountain When She Comes," and "Michael, Row the Boat Ashore." Each of the oldies opened memories inside Ricky, and the memories hurt.

He sat down on the top step of the porch and wondered if there was a moon in the sky and whether dry lightning accompanied the distant rumbles of thunder. After a while, King began to howl. Sol quit his harmonica playing, and the front door squealed open.

"Dumb dog doesn't know a good musician when he hears one," Sol complained. The porch shook under his weight, and then Ricky felt the man sit down beside him. "How're you doing?"

"Okay." Ricky could heard King pacing nervously in back of the cabin. "What's the matter with that dog?"

"There's a full moon out, and the forest is full of new sounds and smells. They probably drive him mad. And then, there are his memories."

"What memories?" Ricky scoffed. "Dogs can't remember. He's just a wild dog. Suppose you can't train him?"

"I think I can," Sol said quietly. "I didn't tell you his whole story, Rick. See, the first family that owned him was a policeman's family. King was being trained as a police dog. The family had one son, a year or so younger than you are now. The boy and the dog loved each other. Then, one winter, the boy went skating on thin ice. The ice cracked and he was drowned."

King stopped pacing and settled down with a grunt. "What happened then?" Ricky asked, interested in spite of himself.

"King tried to save the boy, but he couldn't make

it. Shortly afterward, his family moved. Perhaps they couldn't take King with them. Perhaps just looking at him was a reminder of their loss, and they couldn't stand it. Anyway, King was sold."

"To the mean guy."

"Correct. To the mean guy."

"Why would someone buy a dog and then mistreat him?"

"I suppose he wanted a really vicious attack dog. But King isn't vicious. It isn't in him. He's turned suspicious, but that's natural with the treatment he got. Even beaten and half starved, kept outdoors in all weathers, cursed and hated, he didn't turn on his owner for nearly a year. When King did go for him, the guy got scared and wanted the dog put down. Luckily I heard about it. With the proper love and care . . . and his memories . . . King will make it."

Sol went into the cabin soon after that. Ricky sat on the porch alone for a while longer, then went to bed. Surprisingly he fell asleep immediately and awoke to the sound of distant thunder. Was it raining? But there was no sound of rain on the cabin roof, and the air was as hot and as dry as it had been yesterday. As he stirred awake he heard Deirdre say, "Sol, shall we forget about going to Lincoln? I don't like the weather forecast. Maybe we shouldn't leave Ricky here alone if there are storms brewing."

"They've been predicting storms and rain for weeks," Sol replied. "It's wishful thinking. And even if it does storm a little, so what? We won't be gone long, and Ricky will be safe here in the cabin. He won't go anywhere!"

"Even so . . . ," Deirdre hesitated, and Ricky got up quickly. He had to make sure they left for town. He didn't want the Gallaghers hanging around baby-sitting him because they were afraid it might rain! Clumsily Ricky pulled on his T-shirt and jeans, fumbled on his sneakers, and made his way to the kitchen.

"Hey, good morning!" he said, trying for a smile. "I smelled the coffee and got hungry. Is it raining out?"

There was pleased surprise in Sol's voice. "Not yet, but it's darkening up, and there are a few thunderheads around. If we're lucky, we may get some rain today."

Deirdre offered him breakfast. He pretended that he was hungry, eating bacon and scrambled eggs and washing them down with coffee.

"Good!" he exclaimed, though the food made his stomach turn. "I'm hungry this morning. Must be the mountain air, or something."

"Could be my good home cooking." Deirdre sounded delighted. "Look, Ricky, are you sure you'll be okay up here? We could put off our trip to Lincoln, really. We have plenty of canned goods."

"No, go ahead." Please, please go, he urged silently. "I'll be fine."

"Well—" Deirdre broke off, and Ricky knew she was looking at Sol. He could almost visualize Sol's shrug.

"He'll be fine," Sol said. "Besides, he's got King to keep him company. If we start now, we'll be back in a couple of hours' time, not much later than two or three o'clock."

"Take your time." For a few hours, Ricky thought, I'll have peace!

The Gallaghers started preparing for their trip. Ricky just wished they would go. He didn't want to keep smiling and playing his cheerful role. Outside, distant thunder growled again, and he could hear King whine.

"I'm leaving King tied to the porch railing," Sol told him. "He's on a long leash, so even if it does start raining, he'll be able to come up onto the porch out of the rain." He paused. "The leash is strong, and so is the collar he's wearing. He won't be able to break loose and get away."

Ricky nodded. Sol was remembering yesterday morning and reassuring him that King couldn't get loose and frighten him.

"There's milk and orange juice in the ice chest, plus some sandwiches for your lunch." Deirdre bent and kissed his forehead. The cool touch of her lips made Ricky think of his mother at the hospital. "Be back soon, Rick."

Ricky kept smiling until he heard the front door

close and the Bronco start up. Then he exhaled a long breath and slumped back into his chair. They're gone, he thought. I hope they take their time. I don't care if they never come back!

He didn't care about anything. It was good to sit there and be limp and without thought. After a while, he got up from his chair and fumbled his way out of the kitchen to the main room. He groped for the lumpy couch and was lying down on it when something hard hit him in the spine. He rooted the object out and realized it was Sol's harmonica. Instantly memories hit him, memories of Leo singing and clowning, of Deirdre laughing, of himself telling the folks about adventures around Bobcat Lake ...

"Damn you!" Ricky flung the harmonica as far as he could. There was the sound of shattering glass, and King began to bark.

"Shut up!" Ricky howled. "Shut up, you big, dumb, stupid dog! Shut up! Shut up!"

He lay back on the couch, exhausted and shaking. Perhaps he slept, because for a long time he neither thought nor felt anything. When he finally stirred, it was because thunder was booming and thudding across the close, heavy air.

"The thunder's a lot nearer," Ricky mumbled, sitting up on the couch. As he spoke, another roll of thunder made the cabin windows rattle. The dog on the porch whined and began to pace, big paws padding and claws making a scratching, annoying sound. "Oh, be quiet," Ricky muttered. "It's just thunder!"

How long had it been since the Gallaghers left? How long had he been asleep? There was no way of telling. Ricky got off the couch and fumbled for his cane. He was thirsty. He would have some orange juice, and then—

Bang . . . crasssshhhh!

4

"This is going to take some time to fix," Ben Anderson said. He ran his hand over the hood of the Bronco, flicked away a bit of mountain dust. "Once the master cylinder goes, that's it for the brakes. You were lucky to get down the mountain in one piece."

"How long will it take to fix?" Sol demanded. The Bronco's brakes had begun to feel mushy just after their descent from the mountain. By the time they had reached Lincoln, he could put his foot on the brakes and feel them go right down to the floorboards. He had had to pump the brakes just to get to Ben Anderson's garage.

"Well, we don't carry the parts for these Broncos, Sol. I'd have to get a new master cylinder from the nearest distributor, which is Boston, I believe. It'll take a couple of days."

"But we've got to get back to the cabin!" Deirdre protested. "We left Ricky there alone!"

"Ricky Talese?" Ben Anderson had been the

owner, chief mechanic, and gas-pump attendant for this station throughout many years, and had got to know the Gallaghers well during the last five summers. At first, he had thought that they were crazy when they rented that mountain cabin way out in the boondocks. What would city folks do in a cabin with four tiny rooms, no running water, phone, or electricity? But the Gallaghers had managed, all right. Ben thought them good folks. They really loved the mountains, and so did those two kids who had come along with the Gallaghers, most summers. It was really too bad about Leo.

"How's Ricky doing?" he asked now. "Can he get around on his own?"

"Not really. Not too well. We left him alone today because we felt we were crowding him too much." Deirdre looked toward the mountains with a worried frown. "I wish we'd brought him along, or not come at all. I had a feeling something was going to happen."

"Nothing's going to happen," Sol soothed. "Look, Ben, can't we call around and see if anyone local has the part I need?" As he spoke, a loud, rumbling peal of thunder rolled overhead.

"Ricky'll be worried if we're late," Deirdre said. "I wish we had a phone. I wish we could get in touch with him. It's going to storm and he'll be caught in the middle of it."

Sol took his wife by the shoulders and gave her a gentle shake. "Come on," he said. "Quit imagining things! Ricky won't worry about us. He's been through storms before, Dee. Remember that one we had a couple of years back? Thunder and lightning and winds like a hurricane. Ricky and Leo loved it!"

"Yes, but . . ." But Leo was with him then. He wasn't alone in the dark.

Deirdre watched as Sol followed Ben Anderson into Ben's little office, and then she looked toward the mountains again. Another boom of thunder made her wince. "That one was closer," she muttered. The sky was turbulent with thunderheads, and the air was hot and stiflingly close. If only it would rain and get it over with, she thought.

Sol came out of Ben Anderson's office. He shrugged and shook his head in answer to her questions. "No, nothing. Ben's putting a call in to Boston right now. He says that we should have the part in a day or two if they send it right out."

"A day or two! Ricky—"

"Relax," Sol said. "We're not going to leave Rick alone for two days! Ben's going to call his nephew and have him drive us up to our place. When the Bronco is fixed, the nephew will drive it to our cabin. That's service!"

"For sure," Deirdre said. She was relieved that

they weren't going to be stuck in Lincoln. It would be hard without transportation, but they would be all right. "When can we leave?"

Sol slid an arm through Deirdre's and guided her out of the service station. "I said, relax. Ben is arranging things. Meanwhile, we have some shopping to do, remember? And I could use some coffee. Driving without brakes isn't my idea of having a good time."

They walked across the street toward a small diner, and as they did so a gash of white lightning slit the sky. It was followed almost immediately by thunder. "That was awfully close!" Dierdre gasped.

"It was miles away," Sol scoffed. "I counted three one hundreds before the thunder came."

Deirdre didn't say anything. She was thinking of Ricky in that cabin alone. Well, not alone . . . worse than alone. There was King, brooding, suspicious. "I wonder," she said slowly, "how King's reacting to the storm? Sol, I wish we were there. I wish we'd never left the cabin!"

Bang . . . crassshhh!

Ricky stood where he was, heart pounding. That one had been close! King began to go crazy, barking and whining and scuffling his nails on the porch floor.

Ignoring the dog, Ricky turned toward the kitchen. He was thirstier than ever. He fumbled for the ice chest, barking his shins, bumping into the camp stove, banging his forehead on a cupboard door before locating the chest. He pulled out the bottle of orange juice from the chest and tipped it toward his mouth.

Smasssh ... crasshhhh!

The bottle of juice fell out of Ricky's startled fingers and smashed all over the floor. He could feel the hairs on the nape of his neck prickle.

"That was right on top of us!" he whispered. A loud, moaning wind had started up, and Ricky could hear it swishing at the branches of the trees. Behind the cabin, the old white pines bent and groaned and heaved.

Suddenly, without warning, Ricky smelled something strange in the air—ozone. That meant the lightning was very near!

"I'm getting out of here!" Ricky gasped. He turned, blundered into the kitchen table, fell, then pulled himself to his hands and knees and began to crawl across the floor.

CRASSSHHHHHHHH!

The last crash was so deafening and horrendous that Ricky didn't notice, at first, the splintering, crackling, splitting sound that accompanied the big bang. When those sounds continued, terror filled him.

"That's not lightning!" he shrieked. "The trees ... the pine behind the cabin ..."

The big white pine tree was falling! Terror made him lunge toward the front door. He felt the wooden door against his palms, fumbled madly for the doorknob, pulled it open. As he crawled onto the porch, a blast of wind nearly knocked him back through the doorway. He could also hear the scrabbling of King's paws on the porch. It sounded as if King was straining at his leash.

"Run, dog!" Ricky shouted. "The tree's coming down on top of us!"

There was a snapping sound close by. Ricky threw up a hand to ward off whatever might be threatening him, closed his fist tightly around something smooth and familiar. King's leash! The dog had snapped a porch rail and was loose!

Next instant, Ricky was pulled down the stairs and down the walkway. He tried to regain his footing, fell, and was dragged through brush and brier as if he were a sack of potatoes.

"Stop!" he shouted. "Stop, you dumb dog! You ..."

Whatever he meant to say was lost in the biggest crash of all. The splintering, thudding, tearing sound behind him could only mean one thing. The old white pine had fallen onto the cabin, demolishing it. If he had been inside one second more, he would have been crushed to death!

5

King kept on running. The weight of the boy clinging to his leash hardly slowed him down.

"Stop!" Ricky yelled. He tried to rein King in,
make him stop so that he could regain his footing,
but it was impossible. The pain of brier and bush
whipping against his face made Ricky want to let go
of the leash, but instinct made him cling to it even
more tightly. King had eyes. King could see what
was happening.

Finally King stopped. Ricky managed to get to his
shaky knees. Thunder boomed, close, but not quite
so close. Ricky could hear King panting. Clutching
the leash tightly, he listened for sounds that might
tell him where they were. King had run quite a distance from the house. Perhaps the dog had dragged
him a hundred yards. The question was . . . several
hundred yards which way?

"Where the heck are we?" Ricky muttered.

The wind was even stronger here, and the trees

moaned and keened around them. More thunder banged. There was still no sign of rain.

"That's good, anyway. We won't drown while we're waiting for the Gallaghers to get back." Then it struck Ricky that other trees might have been downed by the lightning storm, trees that might block the mountain road to the cabin. If that were the case, the Gallaghers might not return for quite some time. He wished now that he had gone to town with Sol and Deirdre.

"They'll get back," he said aloud, to calm himself. "When they hear the thunder, they'll turn back. It wouldn't surprise me a bit if they're—Hey! Stop, you stupid dog!"

There was another crash of thunder nearby. King bolted again, nearly tearing Ricky's arm out of its socket. "Stay!" Ricky yelled, trying to haul on the leash. "Cut it out!" But the dog was racing again, and Ricky was knocked off balance, was pulled along the ground while branches exploded in his face and whipped across his arms and body. He didn't even have the wind left to shout for King to stop. He tried to rein King back, but the dog ran even faster, and Ricky was tumbled along behind him, deafened by the thunder and the now ferocious wind.

Smack! Something struck Ricky square in the face, making him gasp with pain. Involuntarily, he loosened his grip on the leash, but tightened it again. King had eyes . . . he didn't. He had to hold on, no matter what. *Had* to!

Finally the dog slowed. Moaning, Ricky felt his raw, smarting face with his torn hands. A huge welt was forming over his eyebrows.

"What hit me?" he muttered. Holding on to the leash with one hand, he groped around him with the other. He expected to feel brush, a sapling, perhaps. Instead, he felt the hard surface of a rock.

"If I'd smashed into that rock, it would have killed me," Ricky groaned. He used the rock as a lever to haul himself to his aching knees. He felt dizzy. A roll of thunder and another gust of wind made him flatten out against the rock.

King yelped and whined. The dog didn't like what was happening. Ricky felt cold, prickling apprehension. Dogs had instincts, and King probably sensed danger. More storm or maybe . . . ? Who knew what? It probably wasn't at all safe here. And where was "here"?

Ricky ran his free hand over the face of the rock. It was huge. Stretching his arm out to its full length, he still couldn't feel the end of it. Rounded in back, flat in front . . . rather like a stone chair. Suddenly recognition hit Ricky, and he laughed in relief.

"It's the Edsel Rock!" he shouted.

The Edsel Rock. Leo had discovered it a couple of summers back, when they were exploring the forest some distance from the cabin. The rock had been in a thicket of young birch and pine and alder, and Leo had said it looked just like a car. Ricky had given it its name, and they had had a lot of fun with it.

"I know this rock like I know my own face," Ricky said. "Here's the left side . . . where the stone's all chipped. I tried to hack my name into the stone, but it didn't work." A thought came to him. "If we're at the Edsel, I'm a long way from the cabin, or what's left of it. They'd never think to look for me out here!"

King tugged on the leash. Ricky pulled back on it, and King growled, but stayed where he was. "I've got to get someplace where they'll find me," Ricky muttered.

But how? Ricky felt around the rock, hoping for . . . what? He didn't really know, until his fingers contacted moss.

"Moss always grew on one side of the Edsel," he breathed. He concentrated, visualizing the tough, gray-green mat of rock-spike moss and the way it turned silvery in the glint of the sun. The *setting* sun!

"This side faces west," he cried. "I *know* it! And if this is west, this has to be east, and that's north and that's south." He repeated these directions a second time, then a third. "I've got to figure it out," he told himself. "I'm not going to hurry."

He thought it out. Blackberry Road, the twisting

dirt road that led up the mountain, ran somewhere southwest of the Edsel Rock. He and Leo had often walked to it, keeping their shortcut a big secret from Sol, who thought he knew all the trails on "his" mountain. Ricky and Leo had blazed several secret trails from the Edsel Rock, often mystifying the Gallaghers by meeting them out on Blackberry Road.

"The road shouldn't be more than a couple of miles from here," he murmured.

Another boom of thunder, accompanied by storm wind, made him move away from the rock. This was the time to leave and try to find his way to Blackberry Road. The storm was moving on. Ricky wished that it had rained, now. He was terribly thirsty. He hadn't had a chance to drink any juice before the lightning bolt hit.

"There's a brook that runs between here and the road," he reminded himself. "I can get a drink there." Even so, he felt hesitant about leaving the familiar spot. "What other chance do I have?" he reasoned with himself. Beside him, the dog panted. "I'll have to rely on you, dog. I don't like it, and I don't trust you, but you have eyes and I haven't."

King made no sound, but Ricky knew he was ready to leave. He could feel the big dog tugging on the long leather leash and hear the dry leaves and pine needles crunch under King's paws.

"Okay," Ricky said. "Let's go!"

They walked slowly, Ricky with one hand wound

into the leash lest a sudden movement from the dog pull it loose. He held his other hand outstretched in front of him, trying to ward off the branches that snapped in his face, but it was no use. When a branch narrowly missed piercing his eyes, Ricky stopped walking. "I need a stick or something. Stay, dog!"

Unwillingly King stopped. Ricky hunkered down, searching the ground for a fallen branch. He found several, but they were either too long, too short, or rotten. Finally he found a branch that was almost the right size. He tried switching it back and forth as they began walking again, but it wasn't much use. Because the weight of the branch unbalanced him, Ricky ended up stumbling and falling every few feet. Worse, without his free hand, he had no defense against the swarm of mosquitoes and flies that had zeroed in on him.

"They probably smell blood," Ricky muttered. His face and hands were covered with scratches and welts.

King didn't help, either. Instead of walking evenly beside the boy, the dog surged ahead or lagged behind or suddenly changed direction, making Ricky fall or walk into trees.

"You must do it on purpose," Ricky muttered. "I know you're doing this on purpose! No dog could be such a moron!"

As they continued to walk, Ricky's thirst became unbearable. The air was hotter than ever, and the knowledge that he was helpless made Ricky's heart pump wildly. All he could pray for was that they were holding a true southwesterly course and that they would stumble onto the mountain stream soon. Ricky bit his ragged lip trying to ignore the buzzing torment of the mosquitoes and flies. He had to keep steady, remain cool. He had to think. If he started to fall apart, he would really be in trouble.

But after a while Ricky's hopes began to crumble. No way could they be going in the right direction! They would have been at the creek by now had their course been true.

"Damn it!" Ricky shouted, yanking King to a halt. He racked his brains, trying to retrace the course he had walked with Leo. Were there any landmarks? They had blazed some trees on the trail, but not too many. Most of their landmarks had been those of sight. It had been so easy in those days. You just said, "Turn east at the big hemlock pine, or, a mile farther than that clump of birch . . ."

"What do I do now?" Ricky asked aloud. "How do I get to that stream? Dog, aren't you thirsty? Don't you have any instincts? Don't dogs know how to sniff their way to water?"

King paced ahead of Ricky, restless and wary. Ricky continued to walk. Swish . . . smack! A tree branch whipped against his shoulder, making him grunt with pain. He couldn't think of the pain now, though. He had to keep going! He had to keep hoping that they were on their way to the stream, the stream with clear, cool mountain water.

King stopped. The suddenness of his halting caused Ricky to lose his balance, and he sprawled out on the forest floor. Why had the dog stopped? Ricky listened intently, but the forest was still. Birds were calling and twittering in the trees, and there was some rustling in the underbrush. Some small animal was nearby, a squirrel perhaps.

"What's wrong with you?" Ricky demanded.

King growled.

"There's nothing to worry about and you know it!" Ricky got to his feet. His thirst and fear made him yank cruelly at the leash. "Let's get going!"

The dog wouldn't budge. Ricky started to haul King along, but the dog snarled so viciously that Ricky dropped the leash. In a moment, the dog might snap at him, bite him!

"Okay," he said shakily. "If you want to stay here, then stay here! I'm going on!" He took a step forward, almost sobbing with frustration. King began to bark. "Shut up! I don't need you! You can go—"

Ricky screamed. The ground beneath him seemed to crumble away. He heard himself shriek once more as he fell into black emptiness.

6

Ricky landed with a jolt. He lay where he was, feeling pain radiate through his feet up to his face and head. For a second, the pain was so bad that he could hardly breathe, and then it eased. Carefully he moved his head, arms, fingers, legs. Nothing seemed broken.

Where was he? Everything around him was silent. King had quit barking. "King!" he shouted, but there was no answering pad of the dog's paws, no whine or snarl or any other sound. The dog had gone. But of course the dog had gone. He had let go of the leash!

"King!" Ricky called again, without much hope. He had to admit that the animal had tried to warn him. The barking, the snarls had been meant to convey a message.

"I was stupid," Ricky told himself. "Now, I'd better quit being stupid and try and get out of this place."

He got to his knees and then to his feet and started to feel around him. From what he could gather, he was in some kind of hole. It wasn't very wide, but it was deep, and the sides of the hole were made of crumbly, dry earth. There was nothing that might give him a handhold and help him climb out.

He tried, anyway, hooking his fingers into the soft earth. It was no use. The soil dribbled away between his grasping fingers, and he fell backward onto the ground. He thought of jumping to try and reach the top of the hole, but even though he jumped as high as he could, he still couldn't reach high enough. Whatever it was he had fallen into was deep, all right.

On his next jump, Ricky fell, hurting his shoulder. He gasped in pain, and at the same time he sat up, listening. He had heard something—a bark. King?

"King!" he shouted.

The barking came nearer, then stopped. He could hear the dog whining above him. King had come back!

"King, good dog!" he exclaimed. He was so grateful for the dog's return that he didn't realize at once that he was still helpless. What could King do for him, anyway? Could the dog lie down and hold out a paw and help him out?

"You needn't have come back," Ricky sighed. He felt suddenly exhausted, and his raging thirst made him want to cry. "Thanks . . . but it's no use. You'd better get along, dog. Maybe if you make it to Black-berry Road and people see you, they'll come look-ing for me."

But that was, of course, a forlorn hope. How would King find his way to the road? They were probably off course, anyway. King would probably just run off and go wild, live with the foxes and coyotes and other wild creatures.

The dog whined, pawing the ground above and sending loose sprays of dry earth down on Ricky.

"Cut that out!" he protested. "You want to bury me alive?" He raised his arms to protect his face from the falling dirt, reached high above him and felt, with the tips of his fingers, something that dan-gled just beyond his reach.

Ricky gasped. The leash! He had forgotten about the leash!

The curl of leather hung tantalizingly above Ricky's fingers. He tried to grasp at it, failed. He fell back again, and the dog barked, drew away.

"King!" Ricky shouted. "Come back! Please come back!"

There was a pause, and then the big dog was back. Ricky could hear King panting somewhere up above him. He stood on tiptoe, trying to find the leash. There. It was there.

"If I was just a couple of inches taller!" Ricky moaned.

Suddenly he fell to his knees on the floor of the

hole and began to scoop dirt into a hill. He tried to keep the loose and crumbling earth together, tried to pound it firm with the flat of his hand.

"Hold, darn you, hold! Don't fall apart on me!" he was almost sobbing. "I just need a couple of inches of height."

Ricky got up on the small pile of dirt. It collapsed just as he was reaching for the leash. He wanted to shout with frustration, but he forced himself to get down on hands and knees again and build another dirt step.

"This has got to work," Ricky muttered. He drew a deep breath. "Ready?" he called. Groping upward, he felt the leather brush his fingertips. "Okay. Now . . ."

He put his weight on the pyramid of dirt, felt it give way, jumped . . . and grasped the leash! King growled, yelped, and began to back away from the edge of the pit. Ricky clung to the leash, trying for a foothold on the sides of the pit. King yelped again. Suppose the leash broke? Ricky fought desperately to push and pull himself up. Now his groping feet found a difference in the texture of the earth. He could feel grass.

He was over the rim of the pit, lying on the ground. "I'm out! I made it!" Ricky gasped.

He felt around with his hands, connected with something huge and rough. A tree . . . a tree lying on the ground. Ricky's probing fingers moved along the tree trunk, felt the tough, ropy sinews of huge roots.

"An uprooted tree!" he exclaimed. Then he shuddered, remembering how he had seen great trees that had fallen and become uprooted. The cavities those trees had left in the ground had been enormous. "So that's what I fell into," he muttered.

Beside him, he could hear King panting. The dog had saved him. Had King known what he was doing, or had he come back by accident, dangled his leash over the edge of the pit by accident?

"Sol said that you tried to help the other boy," Ricky murmured. His heart was pounding hard. "Is that why you came back for me? But that's impossible. Why should you try and help me?"

Whatever the truth, Ricky knew he would never call King "stupid" again! "You saved my life down there," he said, extending a hand. "Thanks, dog."

King growled deep in his throat. It was an obvious warning—hands off! Ricky snatched back his hand and the growling stopped.

"Okay, so you don't want to be friends!" he exclaimed. Still, it was hard to resent King or to be angry with him. King had gotten him out of that hole, perhaps saved his life. How long could he have stayed there without food or water?

"Water," Ricky murmured, overwhelmed with thirst. He got to his knees. "We'd better get going, dog."

King didn't obey Ricky immediately, but hung back a second. It was as if he were saying: "I'm moving because *I* want to, not because you want me to."

They began to walk again. Ricky had lost all track of time. He wished that he had his special wristwatch with him—the one his parents had given him soon after his accident. He had always hated the thing as a constant reminder of hours spent in blindness and had never worn it.

He had also lost all sense of direction. East, west, north, or south—he had no idea which way they were headed. He only knew that he was terribly thirsty and that his throat was almost closed with dryness. Once, he tried the old trick of putting pebbles into his mouth to raise saliva, but this didn't help. He chewed the leaves of the trees that whipped against him, but the bitter leaves only made his thirst worse. Tired and aching and weak, he stumbled and fell more and more often, banged up against trees, smashed into low-hanging branches.

He didn't even have the strength to fight off the insects that swarmed about him, buzzing and humming and stinging. As he stumbled and groped along, Ricky's tired mind began to catalog the kinds of flies that lived in these parts.

"Blackfly and deerfly and humpbacked blackfly ..." Over and over in his mind, the words came and went. "Blackfly and deerfly and humpbacked blackfly." Wasn't King thirsty, too? He could hear the dog panting nearby.

"I have no idea where we are," he told the dog. "I don't know where we're heading, either. Maybe it's so dry here that the creeks have all dried up."

The thought of that creek was maddening! It was agony thinking about water. Ricky remembered how he and Leo had skipped stones in the water, splashed each other. The taste of sweet, clean mountain water flooded Ricky's memory and made him giddy with want.

Suddenly he stopped, tensed. Was he hallucinating? "King, do you hear it?" he whispered.

The dog didn't stop walking. He moved ahead, tugging Ricky along. Heart thumping, adrenalin pumping energy into his tired muscles, Ricky followed. Water. Was he really hearing water? Surely that was water splashing on rocks. He sobbed. Nothing sounded like that except water.

"King, it has to be water! It has to be . . ."

The dog quickened his pace. King was almost trotting. Ricky tried to run, fell, got up, and stumbled again. King surged ahead, and the leash tore from Ricky's hand. Half sobbing, cursing, the boy crawled along the ground, feeling pine needles and dry grass and brier cut into his hands. Then the underbrush gave way. Ricky could feel smooth stones. The sound of water was very near.

Splash! Ricky gasped as he tumbled into the water.

He lay where he was, stupefied at the wonder of the cool wetness. He sucked it into his mouth and nose, coughed, laughed, and sat up shouting with joy.

"We found it! We found it! Yeahhh!"

He shoved his face into the water, drinking, sucking in as much water as he could. In the distance he could hear King lapping away.

"I did find it after all!" Ricky exulted. Somehow he had managed to chart a true course that had led to water. He didn't know when he had felt this good about anything. "It just took long because of that hole in the ground . . . and because I couldn't see where I was going," Ricky said. "I guess we came here the roundabout way. But I found us water! Now, we can head toward Blackberry Road."

He stopped talking to bury his face in the water again. His cuts and welts and bites stung, but it felt so good! Ricky wanted to tear off his clothes, sneakers, and socks and jump into the water, but thought better of it. Even though the stream was shallow as far as he could remember, he wouldn't be able to see stones on the stream bed. With King tugging, he might trip and fall and knock himself out.

In the distance, he could hear King taking a dip, shaking and splashing. "Feels good, doesn't it?" Ricky called. He felt good enough to be friendly.

Now he sat on the creek's edge, letting his feet dangle into the water, relaxing. He wanted to rest, let his muscles and wounds have a chance to heal. The only problem was that he was hungry. Breakfast had been a long while ago, and he hadn't eaten a thing since. Besides, the unaccustomed exercise had built up his appetite. If only there was something to eat!

Then he remembered the duck bread in his jeans pockets. Maybe some of the bread was still there! He jammed a hand into his pants pockets and exulted as he pulled out a handful of bread. He was hungry enough to gulp it all down! He started to cram the stale, dry bread into his mouth.

A panting, woofing sound not too far away made him stop. King has eyes, he told himself. Let him find his own food! But somehow this thought seemed so poor-spirited and mean that Ricky was embarrassed. He broke the bread into two pieces, whistled.

"King! Come and get it!"

There was a pause in the dunking and shaking and splashing sounds downstream. King had heard the chow call.

"It's not steak or anything, but it's food," Ricky shouted. "Come and get it, King, old boy!"

Ricky waited. He could hear the padding sounds of King's approach, and then there was silence. He held out King's share of the bread. Would the dog come and get it? He whistled again. And then King growled.

It was a low, warning growl, and it made Ricky's scalp crawl. Then indignation washed over him.

"Why are you growling, you flea-bitten mutt?" he shouted. "I'm sharing my bread with you! If you don't want it, I'll eat it myself!"

The dog growled again. King wasn't coming any closer, and those sounds he made weren't friendly! A thought came to Ricky. If King wanted to get the bread, he could take it . . . yes, and Ricky's, too! He leaned back and threw the dog's share as far away from him as possible. He heard the big animal jump and pounce, and then crunching sounds. King was enjoying his supper.

"The only reason I'm feeding you is that I need you," Ricky said resentfully. He began to eat his own portion of bread, then grimaced. Dry bread sure didn't taste too good! He thought of all the delicious food he had been passing up lately—cold chicken, potato salad, pancakes, bacon and eggs. The thought made him hungrier than before, and he quickly swallowed the last of the dry duck bread. Tasty or not, the bread would give him energy to walk the few more miles to Blackberry Road.

"Once I get there," he said, "I'm home free."

He knew that he should get up and start walking, but it felt so good to rest! He stretched his aching body out beside the creek, yawned with weariness.

"It won't do any harm to rest for a second," he murmured drowsily. "Just a little rest . . ."

His eyes closed, but before he slept he thought of King. The big dog was loose. How do I get him to come to me when I'm ready to go? Ricky thought fuzzily. I should get up and call him now. I really should get going. I . . .

Before he could complete the thought, Ricky was asleep.

7

A few drops of rain began to fall as Sol and Deirdre reached the diner. The air was hotter than ever, but Deirdre shivered.

"Worrying about Rick?" Sol asked.

She nodded. "We shouldn't have brought either King or Rick to the cabin," she replied. "King's still suspicious and unfriendly and Rick's afraid of him. Cooped up there in the cabin with this storm—"

A spear of lightning flashed, and the lights went out in the diner. Almost simultaneously there was a crash of thunder that shook all the windows.

"Now *that* was close," Sol observed. "Wonder where it hit?"

They found a seat near the diner window. More lightning flashed and a strong wind began to whirl the dust and debris down the dusty street. A waitress fumbled her way over to the Gallaghers' table.

"Dry lightning storm," she said, nodding to the

electricity sizzling through the dark sky. "Bad news, after this dry spell we're having! What'll you folks have? We can't cook anything without electricity, but the pie's good and the coffee's hot."

They ate their pie and drank their coffee in silence. The whole diner seemed silent. There were several people there, but none of them spoke as they watched the skies. Finally the storm began to ease, and the lights came back on. Sol nodded to Deirdre.

"Ready to get our shopping done, Dee? Ben's probably found his nephew by now." He spoke casually, but Deirdre knew Sol was as worried about Ricky as she.

They hurried through their shopping and walked quickly back to Ben Anderson's garage. There they found Ben talking to a tanned youngster in frayed cutoff shorts and T-shirt.

"This is my nephew Kenny," Ben said. "He's got himself an old jeep, and he'll run you up to your place whenever you want."

"We really appreciate it," Sol said, and Kenny gave them a cheerful grin. "Can we get started right away?"

Kenny's jeep was parked in back of the station. It was an old model, lovingly repaired and colorfully decorated with a green dragon, a spider, and a ring of fire. As Kenny pulled the jeep away from Lincoln, the Gallaghers saw a distant stab of lightning toward the west.

"Storm's moving off pretty quickly," Kenny said, nodding westward. "We got quite a pounding, though. Heard on the radio that Franconia Notch really got hit bad. And I guess a couple of big ones fell on the Loon Mountain area."

Sol squeezed Deirdre's hand firmly. "Summer storms come and go," he said. "I can't remember a summer when we haven't had at least one lightning storm."

"Yeah, but this is a bad time for dry lightning," Kenny said. "I'm studying forestry at UNH, and one thing we hate is dry lightning in a drought. One good bolt of lightning and a whole forest can go up in smoke."

Sol tried to change the subject. "You the artist who decorated this jeep?" he asked. Kenny began to describe the significance of the spider, the dragon, and the ring of fire. He was still talking when he frowned and slowed the jeep.

"Hey, look up ahead!" he exclaimed.

A roadblock had been set up on the highway, and a group of state troopers were waving motorists back.

"What's going on?" Deirdre asked worriedly.

Kenny stuck his head out of the jeep window. "What's happening, officer?" he called.

A state trooper answered. "Trees are down up ahead . . . road crew is clearing them off the road, but it'll take some time before that's done. Best you folks can do is turn around and head back to town. You could take an alternate route from there."

"I know another way up your mountain," Kenny soothed before Deirdre could say anything. "It'll take a bit longer and it's really a terrible road, but it'll get us to your cabin. It might take the ground crew hours before they get the highway cleared."

He turned the jeep around and joined the long line of motorists heading back toward Lincoln. Deirdre said nothing, but her eyes kept turning back to look up the highway. The dirty gray sky looked ominous. It bothered her.

After a while of silent riding, Kenny switched on the radio. The blast of rock music made Sol wince, but Deirdre was glad of the music. It was so loud that it kept her from thinking of Ricky. Suddenly the music died and an announcer's voice broke in.

"We interrupt this program with an emergency bulletin," the announcer said. "Travelers on the Kancamagus Highway, Route 118, and Route 112 are warned to be on the lookout for roadblocks in certain areas. Trees have been felled by the storm and are blocking traffic."

Sol reached out and turned the radio volume up. The announcer's voice now seemed to boom and echo through the jeep.

"Also as a result of the storm, reports just in indicate that ranger stations in the White Mountain National Forest area have spotted several lightning-strike fires. Keep tuned to this station for further information."

Deirdre reached for Sol's hand, clung tight. There was fire in the mountains!

8

Ricky woke with a start, disoriented and afraid. How long had he been sleeping? He listened to the sounds around him—the lapping sounds the water made, the rustles in the brush.

"What time is it?" he muttered. "I just meant to rest for a little bit."

He sat up, turning his head from side to side and trying to orient himself. "King?" he cried. There was no answering pad of paws, no whine nor bark. "King?" he shouted again.

Where was that dog? He called King again, but nothing happened. Ricky felt furious and frustrated. Damn that dog! Had King just stuck around for food and water before taking off on his own?

A coyote howled, far in the distance, and the sound was eerie and haunting. Maybe King had heard that howl, too, and had gone to join the coyotes. Ricky hated King. Yes, he hated him! How right he had been not to trust that treacherous, mean, vicious canine! The dog had left him here ... abandoned him!

"I'm alone," Ricky whispered. Saying the words made him feel worse. He was blind, helpless, and alone. The good feelings he had had before disappeared, leaving a tense, hard feeling in the pit of his stomach.

"I'll be okay," Ricky quavered. "I'm near water. I'm okay as long as I stay by water. People have lived on water alone for days. They'll find me."

He crawled to the side of the creek, bent down to drink. The water didn't taste as sweet as it had before. He was hungry, and the growling of his stomach made him hate King even more. If that traitor dog hadn't taken off, maybe they would have made it to Blackberry Road! Well, there was no use thinking about ifs. Ricky knew he had two options. He could stay by the stream, or he could try to find the road on his own.

He decided to explore the area a little. Perhaps he could find some landmark that would point him in the right direction. Perhaps, in the morning, the heat given off by the rising sun would show him where east was.

"I'm not helpless just because that dog went off and left me," Ricky told himself.

He started to crawl around, investigating with hands and nose and feet. There were some cattail reeds growing near the creek, and, a little distance away, underbrush and bone-dry grass and bushes. He felt the bushes, prodding, poking with his fingers until he found a cluster of berries.

"I wonder what kind of berries these are?" Ricky murmured. He hesitated, then shrugged. "Here goes nothing!"

He put the berries on his tongue ready to spit them out if they tasted bitter. Instead, wonder grew.

"Blueberries!" he exclaimed. He started to cram the berries into his mouth, delighting in the sweet-tart taste, spitting out leaves and bits of branch. He was gathering another handful when knowledge hit him.

"Blueberries never grew by the creek. Leo and I never found any, and we went all over the place!" A horrible thought hit him. "The other stream . . . all the way over on the other side of Blackberry Road! It's a mile or two from the lake. Is that where I am?"

How had he gotten so mixed up? This was nowhere near the road. Bobcat Lake was far away from everything!

"I'm lost," Ricky cried.

Still clutching his blueberries, Ricky sank down on his heels. He had been afraid before, now he felt panic. With eyes, he could easily have found his way from this stream to Bobcat Lake, and then made his way back to the cabin or to faraway Blackberry Road. Without sight . . . Panic bubbled through him, and he felt nauseated.

Then panic was frozen, swallowed by a greater fear. He heard something—

Something that turned the other night noises to stillness made him catch his breath in terror. He had heard, nearby, a growl that ended in a feral hiss. The menacing sound was accompanied by a strong, musky odor. Noise and odor came from within a few feet of where he knelt.

The snarling, spitting hiss came again. Ricky, crouching by the blueberry bushes, felt cornered. What should he do? What could he do? Whatever it was that menaced him could see him, could easily countermove and attack him no matter what he did.

What, in these parts, would ever attack a human? Bobcats were usually shy, kept out of the way. As for bears, they didn't growl like this, or smell like this. Ricky's thoughts tumbled over one another.

That smell. "It's a fisher," Ricky whispered, remembering.

Fishers were small, maybe forty inches long, maybe twenty pounds in weight. They were like weasels, deft and cunning and swift, tenacious, and deadly when cornered. Maybe this was a female that thought Ricky was a threat to her young. Whatever the reason, this animal had been frightened into attacking.

Ricky tried to move back, heard again the hissing growl.

He crouched, remembering what a fisher had done to a porcupine he and Sol had found once. The fisher's teeth had ripped the animal apart! Sol had told Ricky that a desperate fisher could leap almost twenty feet high—that he had seen a cornered fisher rip up two hunting dogs, kill them, and get away.

"Get away from me!" Ricky shouted.

There was a loud rustling in the underbrush. The fisher was getting ready to spring. Ricky screamed.

Something brushed by him, and he went over backward, sprawling into bushes that entangled him and kept him from rolling over on his stomach to protect face and throat. He shouted again, flailing in front of him with both arms. Then he heard a growling, snarling sound nearby—a different sound from the fisher's hissing. Was he being menaced by *two* wild animals? He managed to sit up. He could hear the low, feral growling of the fisher and the sounds made by the other beast. Now there was a thrashing, crashing noise, a yelp of pain.

A yelp. "King?" Ricky whispered.

Could the big dog have come back? Ricky got to his knees. He would have given anything for his eyes right then. He would have given the rest of his life for one second's eyesight!

"What's happening?" he cried. "What's happening?" Fear and frustration seethed through him as the snarling and crashing continued. Then there was the sound of something scrambling up a tree. The fisher had headed for the trees!

King was making a loud racket, barking and snarling and yelping. Ricky whistled, calling the dog. After a moment, he heard the crunch of dry grass beneath King's paws and the low woof of the dog sneezing.

"You came back!" Ricky exclaimed. "You did come back!"

The dog sneezed again. Ricky sensed that King was nearby. He held out a hand, felt fur at the end of his fingertips. He froze, almost snatched back his hand, but King stood still without a snarl or snap. Ricky drew a deep breath. He knew that animals could sense fear. He must not show King that he was at all afraid.

Using every bit of courage he could squeeze together, he moved his hand an inch forward, stroking the dog's fur. It felt damp.

"Good dog," Ricky said, and then repeated, "Good dog!"

King remained still. More firmly Ricky ran his hand over King's back.

"Why'd you take off in the first place?" he asked softly. "And why did you come back? Did you know I was in trouble? Is that why you came?"

Suddenly the dog yelped. The sound was so unexpected that Ricky literally jumped, his heart pounding violently. It took him a few seconds to realize that the noise King had made wasn't one of warning, but of pain. Ricky remembered what Sol had said about fishers having vicious, needle-sharp teeth.

"Come here, King." He reached for the dog instinctively. The big shepherd didn't move closer, but he didn't move away, either. Ricky felt the big dog tremble as he ran his fingers over King's back. King was shaking. Was he afraid . . . or hurting?

"Be easy, boy," Ricky murmured soothingly. Gently his fingers probed the big, stiff-furred body. Over the back, the neck . . .

King growled. Ricky tensed, but King didn't make any other sound or movement.

"So that's where it hurts," Ricky said aloud. "I wish I could see what's the matter."

He frowned, considering. He knew that even tame dogs, house pets, snapped and bit if you handled them after they had been hurt. That was natural. They figured you were just going to hurt them some more. But he couldn't leave King alone. A fisher's bite was deep, and there wasn't much blood. That meant that the fisher's teeth could have left infection deep inside the wound. He had to draw the poison out, somehow, or there could be severe infection.

Ricky tried to remember what Sol had done for the other hurt animals he was always bringing home to the cabin. There had been birds with broken wings, a squirrel with a gash in its side, and that other squirrel, the one with deep bites in its haunch.

"Sol used hot compresses to draw the wound," Ricky muttered. "He used tea bags to make a kind of poultice. Where the heck could I get tea out here?"

The thought of tea, and black, fragrant coffee, temporarily sidetracked his thoughts. King, moving restlessly, brought him back to reality.

"I think Sol said something about mud," he said slowly. "Sol said that wet mud works when there's nothing else to draw the poison. All right, we've got nothing else. The fisher bit you where you can't even lick the wound."

How was he going to get King down to the creek? Where was the creek, anyway? He reached for the leash, found it swinging from King's collar, gave it an experimental tug. King stayed where he was.

"Listen, you dumb beast!" Ricky exploded. "Do you want to die of gangrene or something?"

This time, King's growl carried all of the dog's old wariness. Ricky frowned. Whenever he raised his voice, King seemed to retreat back into growling hostility. Yet King had allowed a soft-spoken Ricky to probe his wounds. Weird. Well, maybe not so weird.

"Did that second jerk—the one who bought you off your first owner—did he yell at you all the time?"

Ricky asked softly. "That's why you get all bent out of shape when I raise my voice, isn't it?"

He took the leash again and called King gently. Very slowly the big dog moved. Pad by pad, he followed Ricky. Ricky, listening to the sounds of water, went in what he hoped was the right direction. It was hard, it was like trying to find his way in the thickest, darkest night. As the water sounds came closer, Ricky turned back to King.

"I'm going to try and wash you and pack mud over that wound. It won't hurt you, it'll feel good," he promised. Even so, his heart was thumping wildly. Would the big dog allow himself to be handled?

Ricky got down on his knees and navigated the remaining few yards to the creek's edge. There he took off his sneakers and socks, and gingerly slid his feet into the water. The pebbles on the creek bottom were slippery. He nearly stumbled and fell, steadied himself on the bank.

"Come on, boy," he coaxed King. "You don't want an infection in the back of your neck. Come in here!"

King was drinking. Ricky heard the loud lapping sounds. He called King again, and then again. After a while, he heard splashing noises. King was wading into the water. Maybe the cool water felt good against the wounds, Ricky thought. Sol had once said that hurt animals sometimes buried themselves in mud, instinctively seeking relief from infected wounds.

"I have to wash you, boy. Steady, now." Ricky cautioned King. "Steady, yourself," he told himself. "Quickly, before you lose your nerve!"

Gingerly Ricky splashed water on the dog and began to wash. He found that this was hard to do with his hands, so he took off his T-shirt, soaked it, and gently dabbed the wounded area with the cloth. This worked better. King stood still. Once he yelped, then growled, but the growl communicated pain, not warning. Somehow it seemed as if the dog sensed that Ricky was trying to help.

When Ricky had managed to get the wounded area as clean as possible, he bent down and felt in the creek bank for cool, smooth mud. This he packed along the scuff of King's neck. He wanted to tie his T-shirt over the mud to make a kind of poultice, but this King wouldn't allow. Ricky had to content himself with packing the mud over the wounded area as best he could.

"I'll do that for you again in a little while," he promised. "I wish I had some disinfectant instead of mud. There's some back in the cabin, and . . . and Mom keeps this big bottle of alcohol in the medicine cabinet at home."

He stopped, remembering the medicine cabinet, the razor blade. How far away that seemed! He thought, I wonder what the folks would think if they could see me now! The thought made him homesick, suddenly.

"Okay, that's the best I can do." He washed and wrung out his T-shirt and put it on. It felt wet and cool against his body.

"Don't shake the mud off, King. I hope it'll do some good."

Carefully he toed his way out of the brook, felt for the bank, and hauled himself up. He was fumbling for his sneakers when King came up on the bank beside him. Ricky felt a fleeting warmth on the back of his hand. He stayed still, shocked.

Ricky could hear the dog shaking himself some distance away. He started to fumble on his socks, thinking, Did King really lick my hand?

"You are a strange one, dog," he said. "I wonder what your life was like . . . before. You know, before that second guy got ahold of you." It was odd, but he had the impression that King was listening, great head cocked to one side. "That first family you had must have really been kind to you," Ricky went on. "I wonder why they went off and left you. Did they blame you because their kid fell through the ice?"

Ricky tied his sneakers, and crawled, on all fours, from the water's edge. He stopped a little distance from the creek feeling exhausted.

"I think I'm going to try and rest a while," he said out loud. "Then, I'll decide what to do." He remembered that this was not the stream he had set out to find, and that he and the dog were probably miles from any mountain road where they could be found and rescued. He pushed despair away and repeated, "I'm going to rest awhile. If I sleep on it, I might find out what to do."

He could hear the dog moving about, pacing restlessly. Ricky wondered whether he should try to get King to come near, tie him up. Then he decided against it.

"King wouldn't let me, and anyway, he came when I needed him," he said drowsily. His heavy eyes were closing again. "You'll be here when I wake up, won't you, boy?"

Ricky was asleep. Soon he began to snore softly. For a while, the big dog stood looking at him, cocking his sensitive ears, snuffing the wind. Then he circled nearer the sleeping boy.

In his dream, Ricky stirred fitfully, half-rolled over, and felt a warmth against his back. Perhaps it brought him comfort, for he slid into a deep, restful sleep.

9

Jake Simon, the fire boss, arrived at the ranger station at a quarter past six and immediately called a meeting of his staff. He had been in constant touch with the situation since four that afternoon, when the first plumes of white smoke had been sighted by a lookout on the fire tower. Now, in spite of efforts to contain the lightning-strike fires, over a hundred acres of forest were burning.

Jake Simon's "office" in the ranger station, now officially called Fire Headquarters, was a small room just off the radio room. Here a large map had been set out on an easel, and Jake's staff crowded around. In the outer room, fire fighters, dressed in yellow fire-retardant shirts and orange hard hats, hurried into waiting vehicles and bulldozers. The dispatcher talked incessantly into the radio mike.

Jakes had just finished listening to a report from Chris Marten, his line boss. "Chris has divided the perimeter of the fire into sectors," he told his staff. "Each sector is manned by the fire fighters working under a sector boss. He's also given us an evaluation of the situation, which isn't good at all."

"It's never good when there's pine and spruce and fir," Chris Marten said. Jake nodded. He had seen pine trees go up like tinder, consumed by their own turpentine. Worse, such trees made for a crown fire, the dreaded forest fire that spread from treetop to treetop. Such a fire could blaze off a hundred acres within an hour!

"Okay," Jake said, "I'd like your feedback now. How shall we fight this one?"

The discussion took precious time. Jake Simon listened to his veteran staff hash out their ideas on how to get the fire under control. That was a fire boss's job. As he listened, his mind was far away and moving with the fire. If a crown fire wasn't contained, it could devastate huge hunks of the National Forest. Given the abnormally dry conditions, and the fact that a fire could create its own hellish winds, they were in for a lot of trouble!

He was listening when a state trooper came into the ranger station, followed by a man and woman. The couple, Jake noted, looked worried and frightened. The state trooper came up to Jake's office and stuck his head inside.

"Sorry to bother you," he said, "but these people have a problem and I think you'd better hear it." He turned to the waiting couple. "Mr. and Mrs. Gallagher, this is Jake Simon. He's in charge of fighting this fire."

The couple exchanged glances. Jake was in a hurry, but he sympathized with the fear in their eyes. "What's the problem?" he asked.

It was the woman who answered. "We rent a cabin up in the mountains near here. We came into Lincoln for supplies this morning, and . . . now all roads leading back to our cabin are blocked."

Jake frowned. "Well, we're doing our best, Mrs. . . . ? I'm sure, in due time . . ."

She shook her head, interrupting him. "You don't understand! It's not the cabin we're worried about. There's a boy up there, all alone. Ricky's blind!"

Ricky dreamed that he was home.

He was glad to be home. As usual, he could see in his dream, and as he ran across the remembered driveway and up the stairs and through the front door he shouted with the gladness of homecoming.

"Mom! Dad! I'm home!"

There was no answer. Ricky looked around, bewildered. Where was everyone? The house looked deserted. Dust lay thick on everything, as if no one had lived in the house for years. Ricky started to run through the house, opening one door and then another.

"Mom! Dad! Where is everyone?"

Finally he came to his own room. The door was not locked, and when he touched the doorknob, the door swung open into darkness. There in the dark-shuttered room, sitting on the bed, was a blind man. His eyes were covered by huge black glasses and one hand clutched the knob of a white cane.

Ricky sat up, wide awake.

What time was it? He couldn't tell. He rubbed sleep from his eyes, trying to shake off the shock of his nightmare, trying to guess the time. Was it close to dawn?"

His stomach growled, and he remembered that he was in trouble. He and King were still nowhere near any place of rescue or safety. And, he was starving! Even counting that dry bread, it was hours since he had eaten last.

"King?" he called.

There was no answering bark. Where had the dog gone now? Ricky wondered irritably. Then he checked himself. "Easy, Ricky." King had to be nearby. If he had wanted to take off, he would have done so a long time ago.

"King!" he called again, and whistled.

Faint and far off, he heard a bark. That was King, all right! "King!" he yelled in relief. "Where the heck are you?"

Now he heard the sound of underbrush being trampled and pushed aside, and King came bounding up to him. Even without eyes, Ricky could sense the dog's pleasure.

"What have you been up to?" he asked. "You took off while I was asleep, dog, and now you show up all pleased and happy!" But he spoke without the edge of irritation in his voice. He was glad King was there. He grinned suddenly. What would Sol say if he knew Ricky was *glad* of the dog's company?

"If we don't get a move on, we'll never know what Sol might say," he told King. "We've got to make plans. We can follow this creek and hope it leads us somewhere, or . . . King? What are you up to?"

The dog was making strange noises. Ricky held out an investigating hand and heard a short, warning growl. Surprised and a little hurt, he lowered his hand.

"What's wrong with you?" he demanded.

King began to make those sounds again. Ricky could hear the big dog settle himself, could hear the dry ferns and grasses crackle as King settled . . . and then, the sounds continued. Ricky soon realized what the sounds meant. King was having breakfast! Ricky's mouth watered, and he shook his head.

"No wonder you're touchy about being handled! Well, don't worry, I don't want your food. I wish you could hunt me up some breakfast, though. Some bacon would be nice, and toast and maybe waffles with syrup."

The dog continued to crunch and tongue his

food. Then there was a pause. Ricky heard King get up, heard the big paws padding toward him. Something fell to the ground in front of him. Then King backtracked to his place of eating.

"Now, what?" Ricky reached out in front of him, fanned his hand in a slow semicircle, and closed his fingers around a sticky, slimy piece of something. "Yecchhh!" He drew his fingers sharply away and held them to his nose. He smelled fresh blood. He realized, suddenly, that King had offered him a bit of breakfast!

Ricky's throat felt suddenly tight. For King to do *that* . . . He remembered how King had nearly taken a hunk out of him a couple of days ago back at the cabin. It seemed as if a hundred years had passed since then.

"Thanks," he said, around the lump in his throat. "I appreciate it, but I can't eat raw meat the way you can. Not yet, anyway. You'd best finish this piece, too, King. You're going to need your strength today. We have to push on."

Where? he asked himself. He had to figure out where they were heading. He already felt light-headed from hunger, and his muscles were stiff and sore. Worst of all was the realization of his helplessness.

"Where?" he repeated out loud.

His empty stomach rumbled again, and he felt suddenly woozy. I have to eat, he thought, and then remembered the blueberry bushes. He began to crawl in what he hoped was their general direction. After some time he found the bushes, but was disappointed when his fumblings and pickings only yielded a scant handful.

Still, a handful of berries was better than none! He began to eat the berries one at a time to make them last. As he chewed, he remembered what he had been thinking last night before the fisher attacked. He had been thinking that blues only grew beside the creek that led to Bobcat Lake.

"If we could only get down to the lake," he murmured. "Sol would think of looking for me there. I know he would! And there's stuff in the lake . . . Maybe we could catch some fish or a frog or two." The thought of devouring a frog made him want to throw up, but if you were hungry, you could eat anything, right?

"The question is how to get down there," Ricky sighed.

How careless he had been of sight when he had had it. All through the many summers spent with the Gallaghers, he had never once thought of memorizing signs with senses other than his eyes. He had always depended on sight.

Well, no use to dwell on that! He swallowed the last berry, wishing there were more. "But there aren't any more," he sighed. "This is the only place where blues grow in these parts. That's why Leo and I blazed that trail . . . so we would find them, and no one else."

He stopped speaking, transfixed by what he had just said.

"The blazed trees!" he yelled. "The blazed trees . . . that's it!"

King started to bark. He had been close by, Ricky realized. Instinctively he reached out to stroke King's flank as he spoke.

"King, we could do it. We could! All we need is luck. Leo and I made a lot of trails all over the mountain. There was that trail from the Edsel Rock to Blackberry Road, and . . . and a lot of other trails! And, King, we made this trail from Bobcat Lake to the blueberry bushes near this creek. We didn't want to forget how to find the blues whenever we wanted a snack! We didn't tell anyone. It was our secret!"

The dog whined, sensing Ricky's excitement. Ricky remembered how he and Leo had sneaked an ax out of Sol's toolbox and how they had made deep blaze marks on trees leading from the blueberry patch to Bobcat Lake.

"Do you get it, King?" he cried. "If I'm right, someplace around here there are trees with notches cut in them! If I can find just one notched tree, I'll bet I can feel my way down to the lake!"

Ricky slipped his hand into King's leash. They would need one last, deep drink before they left the creek. He fumbled his way to the edge of the creek and there applied more mud to King's injured neck. Then back they went to the blueberry bushes and beyond them into the forest.

"The forest is where we want to go," Ricky muttered, wincing as branches whipped his face and arms. "But, which way do we go first?"

His brief elation faded, leaving him suddenly dizzy and weak. He reached out for support, felt a tree trunk under his hand. Quickly he groped down the gnarled trunk. It was smooth. There was no trace of marks from ax or knife.

"Nobody said it was going to be easy," Ricky said firmly. "Come on, King. We've got to keep on trying. It's a long shot, maybe, but it's the only chance we've got!"

10

A blind boy alone in a remote mountain cabin! Jake Simon groaned.

"How old is Ricky?" he asked. "Is he your son, uh, Mrs. Gallagher?"

Deirdre shook her head. "Ricky's fifteen, and, no, he's not our son. He's like a son." She fell silent, the tears brimming in her eyes, and Sol continued her thought.

"He's like our own, Mr. Simon. He's recently been blinded and is pretty helpless. And he's not alone. There's a German shepherd. Guess we're not making much sense," he apologized, "but we've been terribly worried. We've spent hours trying to find a way back to the cabin, and then we finally went to the police. They suggested we come up here and tell you our problem."

Jake beckoned the Gallaghers into his office. "Can you pinpoint the location of your cabin on this map?" he asked.

Sol concentrated on the large map, then pointed. Jake and his staff breathed easier. There wasn't any immediate danger to the boy . . . not from fire, anyway. The Gallaghers' cabin was on the outer ring of Sector F, where a spot fire was now reported under control.

"I'm sure Ricky is in no danger at all," Jake said, "but just the same, we're going to get him down here as soon as we can." He turned to the radio dispatcher. "Can you find out how the tree removal is coming along? If Blackberry Road is still blocked, we can cut across through Sector F."

There was a spurt of static from the radio. "It won't be long, Mr. Simon. Maybe an hour at the outside."

"Fine. As soon as that road is cleared, I want someone to take a vehicle up to these people's cabin and get the boy out." He smiled at the Gallaghers. "And the dog, too, of course."

"Be careful," Deirdre said. "The dog isn't used to people. He may be hard to handle."

"Not if I go along with your people," Sol put in. "Please. I'd like to. Ricky must be worried by now, and strangers coming might upset him."

"We'll do it that way, then." Jake Simon nodded to the map. "I've got some work to do right now, but I don't want you folks to worry. Why not find a seat and have some coffee . . . relax for a while? We'll get Ricky down for you."

As Jake Simon turned back to his fire-fighting staff, Deirdre took Sol's hand.

"Thank God he's not in danger from the fire," she whispered.

He smiled down at her, some of the worry easing from his eyes. "You see? It's going to be okay. I'll go up and get Ricky, and, hey! I'll bet by the time we get down here, he'll feel like the hero of an adventure story."

There was a pot of coffee and some Styrofoam cups in a corner of the radio room. The Gallaghers poured themselves cups of the strong coffee and sat down to wait.

It was a long wait. It was nine o'clock before news came over the radio that Blackberry Road was clear of fallen trees.

Jake directed a jeep to go up to the Gallaghers' cabin and bring Ricky down. Sol patted Deirdre's hand.

"We'll be back in no time," he told her.

Deirdre tried hard to believe him. She forced herself to think of ordinary things, such as what they would eat and where they would sleep when Sol brought Ricky down from the mountain. And there would be King, too. Could they find a kennel for King at this time of night? If not, a motel would have to do. They would find a motel that took pets and call Ricky's folks from there. If the Taleses heard about the forest fire, they would be worried.

Time inched by. Sitting on the uncomfortable folding steel chair, Deirdre checked her watch every ten minutes and saw nine turn to ten, then to eleven, then to midnight.

"Excuse me," she said to the radio dispatcher, "do you think something's wrong? That jeep left three hours ago. It doesn't take that long to get to our cabin and back."

"Could be the roads weren't really clear, ma'am, in which case they'd have to stop to clear debris away." The dispatcher leaned over his mike. "I'll call them on the radio for you, though."

The radio sputtered as the dispatcher spoke into it. Then he frowned as an answer came across the wires. Deirdre couldn't catch much of the reply.

"What's wrong?" she demanded.

"Apparently they just reached the cabin. There's been an accident." All of Deirdre's blood seemed to freeze as the dispatcher continued, "They say one of the trees in back of your cabin collapsed and fell onto the cabin, crushing it."

That old while pine! "And ... Ricky?" she gasped.

"The jeep driver and your husband are searching the cabin right now. They'll get back to us, Mrs. Gallagher."

Deirdre sat down, feeling weak in the legs. The cabin crushed. And Ricky ... Oh, please, no, she prayed silently. Let Ricky be all right!

The radio crackled again, and the dispatcher

leaned forward to listen. "No trace of the boy or dog anywhere in the cabin!" he reported, relief in his face and voice. "They're going to look for him now. Don't you worry, ma'am. He can't have strayed very far. They'll find him!"

Nothing had ever been this hard before. Ricky found himself walking more and more slowly. Convoys of mosquitoes and flies attacked him, and tree branches lashed at him. Often he stumbled and fell, and each time he fell it became harder to get up. He didn't even know why he bothered to keep on. It was ridiculous. How could he ever find those trees, blazed so long ago?

Perhaps he kept on because King walked beside him, heeling close to the boy now, no pulling in front or lagging behind. Ricky sensed a steadiness in the dog's presence, and it kept him moving.

"I don't know why you stick to me," he said. "I don't know where I'm going. I don't know where I'm leading us."

The dog made no sound, but Ricky knew King was watching him.

"If your first family had kept you, you'd be a different dog, wouldn't you?" Ricky murmured. "I wonder what you were like as a pup, King? I wonder what the other kid was like, you know, the one who went under the ice."

He frowned, thinking of what King must have

endured after his young master's death, and later, at the hands of his bestial second owner. Sol hadn't said much, but Ricky could imagine King shivering outside in the winter, broiling outside in the summer heat, being kicked and cursed and starved. Fury filled him as he thought of that brute mauling and abusing his dog.

"I'd have bitten that jerk's hand off," he told King. "No wonder you went for him!" Then he added, "I'd have given up if I were you. Know that? I'd have given up and died."

He held out a hand, found the shaggy head close to his side. He stroked it. The dog didn't tense or move away, but seemed to lean closer. Running his fingers through the smooth, short fur, Ricky muttered, "You hung on and you survived. You're stronger than I am, you know that? It's really funny, King."

Funny that just a few weeks ago he, Ricky, had been thinking of ways to kill himself and end it all! Funny that he was now struggling and straining to keep going, that he was hoping for rescue.

The thought made Ricky tired. He was so empty and sore, and he wanted to sit down and rest. He was sleepy, and his head was turning cartwheels from hunger and fatigue and the pain and itch of all his bites and scratches and welts. He leaned his head up against a large tree and closed his eyes.

"Just let me rest for a second, King."

But the dog wouldn't let Ricky rest. He whined, tugged at the leash. There was uneasiness in the sounds King made, a sense of urgency that got to Ricky.

"Okay. Okay. I'm coming," he sighed. He pushed himself away from the tree and, hands outstretched, started forward again. He figured that he had one chance in a zillion of ever finding the blazed trees, and maybe King thought so too. He whined again uneasily, as if he could sense and smell something the boy could not.

As if there was some danger close at hand, some danger that Ricky could not see.

Back at Fire Headquarters, Deirdre was still waiting. As the minutes slid into hours, her nerves tautened, stretched till she was sure she would start screaming. Whenever she heard the sound of wheels outside the ranger station, she would leap to her feet and run to the door. Two o'clock came and went, and there was no word from Sol.

Then, at three thirty, Sol stumbled through the door. Deirdre took one look at his face and began to tremble.

"You didn't find him. You didn't . . ."

"No." Sol crossed to her and put his arms around her. His face and hands were scratched and bloody, and he looked exhausted and worried sick. "We used the loudspeaker, and called and called. Nothing! We searched all over the area, using our flashlights. It's too dark to really look carefully, so we decided to come down and try again at first light."

Deirdre clenched her fists. Where could Ricky be? Had he been hurt by the falling tree? Had he crawled off someplace to hide? Was he badly hurt? Could he even be . . .

"Don't think it!" Sol said sharply. "He's going to be all right, Dee. I'm going to ask Jake Simon for help. With a group of volunteers, we could—"

Sol broke off as the radio dispatcher got to his feet. "Mr. Simon!" he shouted. "Mr. Simon, it's Chris Marten." As Jake Simon hurried over to the radio, the dispatcher continued, "That fire in Sector F is burning out of control. Wind shift. He's afraid it might splinter out."

Deirdre and Sol looked at each other. The perimeter of Sector F was near their ruined cabin.

11

Ricky felt heat on his shoulders and back as he walked. The sun had come up sometime ago, and it was now so hot that he would have liked to take off his T-shirt. He might have done so if it weren't for the mosquitoes and blackflies. They droned around him, attacking his face and ears and neck, feeding on yesterday's bites and scars. Ricky's face felt like a swollen mass of bites and welts.

"How are you doing, King?" He reached out for the dog, gently probing the injured neck. The mud pack he had applied back at the creek had long since slid off, but when he lightly fingered King's wounds the dog showed no pain. Maybe the wounds wouldn't fester after all.

"Are you getting bitten, too?" Ricky went on. The dog padded beside him, silent, occasionally snapping his jaws at pests that flew too close.

Suddenly Ricky stopped, listening. "King! That's a helicopter! Listen to it chopping away up there!" Hand on the dog's head, Ricky strained his ears. He willed the copter to come nearer, but the sound was very distant. "Sounds like it's just flying around in circles," Ricky murmured. "I wish it'd come this way and get us out of here."

King whined. The uneasiness in King's whine worried Ricky.

"Listen . . . ," he began.

Suddenly King exploded into sharp barks. Ricky stood stock-still, not knowing whether to move or run or just stay put.

"King, what is it?" he demanded. "What's the matter?"

Something large crashed through the underbrush, blundered past them, and thrashed into more underbrush. Ricky laughed shakily.

"You dummy. . . . That was just a deer, I'll bet! Sounded like he was in a hurry to get someplace!"

They went on. Above them, Ricky noted, the cronk-cronk of ravens, the chitter of starlings, and the flutter of wings. "I wonder what's going on," Ricky said. Even the squirrels sounded agitated. He could distinguish the chirrr-ing sounds they made.

King yelped. Whatever was happening did not please King.

"I wish you could talk," Ricky sighed.

As they plodded through the unquiet forest, Ricky caught his foot in a tree root and stumbled. He came to the ground with a bump hard enough to shake him all over, and he lay still for a moment feeling sick and dizzy. I'll lie here for just a second, he thought.

Then he heard it. Close by and menacing, the raspy, dry rattling made him gasp. Rattler! he thought. Instantly his weariness disappeared as adrenalin pumped energy into him. I've got to get away, got to move.

Move where? Move how? He couldn't *see* the snake! He could walk right onto the coiled, scaled body, right onto the diamond-shaped head and ready fangs! He tried to stay as still as possible. Perhaps if he stayed quiet and motionless, the snake wouldn't bite!

King exploded into barks. Wow-wow-wow! Deep, challenging woofs broke the silence. King was some distance from where Ricky lay. What was the dog trying to do? Is he trying to draw the snake away from me? Ricky wondered.

Again King barked, and then there was silence. In the inexplicable, eerie quiet, Ricky listened for the rattles to sound their dry warning. There was nothing. King barked again. The dog was nearer this time. And then Ricky felt a cold nose pressed against his shoulder. King nudged him urgently. Get going, Ricky, hurry up!

"The snake!" He felt alternating waves of hot and cold, and he was so sick he wanted to throw up. "I might walk into that snake. I can't move, King. Leave me alone!"

King nosed him again. Ricky knew that the dog would keep on doing this until he got to his feet. King was trying to tell him something. Could it be that the rattler had gone? Ricky moved his leg a little bit, expecting to feel the rattler's fangs strike home. Nothing happened. He moved his other leg, then managed to sit up.

"Did the snake go away?" Ricky wondered. "Did you scare it away, King? But rattlers don't act like that. At least, I don't think they do!"

An explosion of bird noise in the branches above him made Ricky turn his blind face upward.

"What's going *on?*" Ricky cried.

He put a hand on King's back, heaved himself weakly to his feet. Lord, he was hungry, and thirsty! Suddenly the realization of what had happened— the fact that he had nearly been bitten by a rattler —hit him. He started to cry. Heavy, dry, aching sobs shook him.

"I hate it!" he shouted. "I hate being helpless. I might as well quit, right now!"

His nerve completely broken, he stumbled a few feet, then went down on his knees. Burying his face in his hands, he wept. After a moment, he felt something pushing against him. King was nudging him again, the cold nose questing against his cheek. King whined softly.

Without fully knowing what he did, Ricky wrapped his arms around the great body. He clung to King and sobbed. He poured out his frustration and helplessness.

"What's the use?" he wept. "What's the damned *use*? We'll never get out of here. We'll never get to the lake. Never . . ."

King began to lick the boy's face, but it was more out of urgency, Ricky felt, than consolation. With Ricky still clinging to him, King began to move. The dog wanted to get out of there. Why? Were there more snakes?

The thought of snakes got Ricky to his feet.

"Okay," he muttered. "I have to calm down. Okay." His body still heaved with dry sobs as he stumbled along, clinging to King's leash.

As he blundered forward, his mind began to wander back to what had just happened. Why didn't that snake just bite me? Ricky wondered. Why is King so darned nervous? Why are the birds making such a racket?

He tripped, nearly fell, and saved himself by clutching at a tree. As he pulled himself erect, he suddenly stopped and began to fumble frantically along the trunk of the tree.

"It is!" he shouted. "It's one of the trees, King! It's one of the blazed trees! I found us one!"

Letting go of the leash, he began to stagger around seeking another tree. He had found that first marked tree, felt the smooth, dry bark and the deep cleft his ax had left in the wood. There were other trees nearby with his mark on them. He knew that now.

Not so helpless after all, Ricky exulted. He reached a second tree, probed it with his hands. There was no mark. Disappointment nearly crushed him, but he fought it down and groped for a third tree.

"King, I sure wish you could help me look!"

The dog was following closely, whining at his heels. King wasn't happy, but Ricky couldn't stop to worry about that now. Arms outstretched, he plunged forward. The rattler was forgotten. He didn't even care whether the snake was waiting for him. He had to find another marked tree!

It took Ricky ten minutes to find another tree with a notch in its trunk. Ten minutes of frustration and pain were forgotten when his fingers explored the notch in that second tree.

"We'll make it now," he whispered. "King, we'll make it."

He forced himself to be calm, to think his next move through. He and Leo had blazed a lot of trees. This being so, this tree could be leading him either to the lake or away from the lake. He had to figure out which.

As he was pondering the problem, Ricky heard the helicopter again. It seemed closer than before.

I wonder if they're looking for us, he thought. They're really far off, now, but if we get to the lake, they're sure to spot us! The thought gave him re-newed energy.

King whined and paced restlessly.

"Okay," Ricky said. "We'll go this way. If we don't reach the lake in an hour or so, we'll have been going the wrong way. There's no way to find out except by trying."

They set out. Ricky cautiously felt for a blaze mark on each tree in his path. They walked for a long distance until a slight incline in the terrain made Ricky stop.

"We've been going the wrong way, King," he said, trying to keep the bitter disappoinment out of his voice. "The lake is down in a kind of valley, so the ground would be sloping down, not up."

They had to backtrack. Ricky was so weary that he felt he could not go on without a momentary rest. But who could rest in all this racket? The birds were still screaming up in the trees, and, as Ricky leaned against a tree, other huge, heavy bodies blundered past them and crashed down the gentle slope. Sud-denly Ricky frowned. He raised his head and sniffed.

"Is there a campfire around here?" he muttered.

He could smell smoke—faint, but unmistakable. If someone had a campfire going, it would explain a lot of things. Campers with jeeps and fires and noisy kids could upset the wildlife. Maybe the birds and the animals in the forest were warning one an-other about a group of unfamiliar, noisy humans!

"I'll bet that's what it is," Ricky said. Then it occurred to him that if there were people nearby, his troubles were over! He raised his voice and shouted, "Hey! He-ey! Is anyone there?"

Birds, shrilling and shrieking, took flight above them. Because I yelled? Ricky wondered, in surprise. He reached out for King, smoothed between the dog's ears.

"Do you think those people are campers? No, I know! They're hunters. That's why the birds are so uptight. They're not supposed to hunt up here," he went on, frowning. Suppose careless hunters mistook King and himself for animals? He had heard of people being killed by trigger-happy hunters!

"Hey there!" he yelled again. "You by the fire! Can you hear me? He-e-ey!"

There was no answer. Ricky shrugged. "Maybe they left camp and left their campfire burning," he said. "It doesn't matter, anyway. I know we're heading for the lake, now, King. Believe me, we're almost home free."

His words were interrupted by a loud booming noise. Ricky gasped, and King began to bark furiously.

"It's okay, boy, okay. It's probably those dummy hunters shooting off their rifles! If the rangers catch them up here . . ."

There was a crackling sound, and, farther off, another big boom of sound. The birds went absolutely crazy. Ricky didn't see how he could blame them. He reached out for the next marked tree.

"We're on the right track. Hey, King. Easy, boy! You're a trained police dog, aren't you? You should be used to firearms!"

There was a sudden gust of wind. It was hot, so hot that it made Ricky draw back. On the wind came a stench of smoke so strong that it left him coughing and gagging.

"That's too much smoke for an ordinary campfire!" he exclaimed. An awful thought occurred to him: Maybe those hunters let their campfire get away from them! Maybe there's a brush fire . . .

Ricky knew that they would have to get to the lake and quickly. A brush fire could spread fast in all this dryness! He fumbled frenziedly for new blaze marks. He didn't walk any more, but practically threw himself from tree to tree. He was feeling more and more light-headed, and the smell of the smoke, stronger now, made him choke and gasp for breath.

I hope the lake's really ahead of us, he thought. I hope I haven't loused things up this time! He broke off the thought as more smoke came to him on the wind. He remembered reading that in a fire you were supposed to keep low, find oxygen at ground level. He dropped down on all fours, feeling for the trees and their markings as he crawled along.

Beside him, King whined, then yelped. Ricky

turned to reassure the big dog, but choked as a layer of dense smoke blanketed him. Smoke filled his nostrils and lungs and throat. He couldn't breathe. He couldn't think. Stunned and nearly senseless, Ricky crumpled to the ground and lay there motionless.

12

"Fall back!"

That was the cry up and down the fire edge in Sector F. "Fall back! Wind shift!"

The wind was now gusting in a westerly direction. Up until now, fire fighters in Sector F had hoped to keep the blaze contained. They had used bulldozers to plow up the ground in a fire line, chain saws to cut down trees. But the fire was making its own unpredictable wind, which howled and blew, whipped up the flames and the smoke, and added its awful noise to the roaring, booming sounds the fire made.

As fire fighters struggled back, pulling out men and equipment in their retreat, the sector boss radioed Chris Marten. Marten was at Sector D, where another unchecked fire was roaring. He listened to the report from Sector F, asked about the velocity of the fire wind and its direction. Then he called Jake Simon at Fire Headquarters.

"The fire's heading straight for Bobcat Lake," he

told the fire boss. "I'm going to need air help, Jake. Can you spare me a chopper?"

Jake Simon frowned. He had just returned from an aerial inspection of the fire area. From a plane, Jake had noted that most of the fires were under control, but that three were still raging, including this one in Sector F. If the Sector F fire spread, there would be real trouble.

"Anyone hurt?" he asked Chris Marten. He listened to Marten's rundown. Several fire fighters had been treated for smoke inhalation, others for burns. New personnel had relieved weary men.

"We managed to pull out all the men and equipment when the wind shifted," Marten continued. "It was a near thing, though."

"I'll get ahold of Air Operations, see what I can do," Jake promised. "Lord knows they have their hands full with this fire, but if possible, I'll get them to send a chopper out to Bobcat Lake. They can fill up the scoop with water and douse the heart of the fire. That'll help."

"Better make it quick, Jake." Chris Marten paused. "Has there been any news of that lost boy?"

"Not yet." Jake frowned, thinking of the search parties that had been combing the wooded area near the Gallaghers' ruined cabin. Since earliest light, volunteers led by Sol Gallagher had combed the woods for Ricky Talese. So far, they had found nothing.

I'd best get those pepole out of that area, Jake thought. I can't afford to have anyone trapped. The wind might reverse direction again, or the fire might crown out. If we don't get that Sector F blaze under control, it might spread through the whole area, destroy everything!

He asked the dispatcher to raise his Air Operations officer on the radio, then walked over to the big map in his office. Revising the zigzag lines that indicated the perimeter of the fire area, he had the thought that a helicopter could do double duty. A copter pilot might be able to spot something that searching parties couldn't see. Hovering over the terrain, a helicopter might find Ricky Talese . . . providing he was still alive.

Ricky lay very still. He couldn't breathe. He was aware that his body was making convulsive attempts to suck in air, but neither his mind nor his body would work. He just wanted to lie there and not move again. He started to black out as another wave of smoke rolled over him.

Then, he felt the pain in his shoulder. Something had grabbed him, was pulling him across the ground. *King,* Ricky's mind registered. He was too far gone for thought, but instinctively his arms and legs made crawling motions, giving the dog some help. But it was no use . . . no use! The smoke was everywhere!

And then, miraculously, the smoke thinned. A gulp of oxygen made Ricky cough and retch. Breathing in air was almost as bad as being without it. He lay in a fetal position, gasping and vomiting and coughing, while King hacked and gagged beside him. How had the dog managed to think under such conditions? Had he remembered his old police-dog training in the emergency?

Some distance away there was the loud, booming sound that Ricky had thought to be a rifle shot. What were those sounds? Whatever they were, they were coming closer. Ricky coughed again as wisps of smoke curled and spiraled around him. King nudged him forcefully.

"I know we shouldn't stay here." But where to go? Where was it safe to go? He felt his shoulder. King had grabbed his T-shirt, tearing it and nipping the skin below. He rubbed the lacerated area. How many times had King come to his aid? But he couldn't sit around thinking about that now!

"We'd better try and get down to the lake," he gasped. "I don't know how big the fire is, but we'd be safer in the water. Like I said before, we're not too far . . . I hope!"

There was another blast of smoke-laden air. Ricky tried to get up on all fours, felt woozy and sick, and collapsed back down on the ground. Another boom sounded . . . pretty close, this time. The noise registered in Ricky's brain, made him remember back to when he had heard a sound like that.

"Back at the cabin," he muttered. "The white pine . . . when it hit!"

The sounds he was hearing came from trees going down!

"Burning trees," Ricky whispered, shocked to stillness. "That has to be it, King. The whole forest around here must be on fire!"

His mind reeled with horror. A forest fire! Forest fires were what you heard and read about, something you never expected to be caught in!

"Got to get to water!" he gasped.

He struggled to his hands and knees and began to crawl. His breath came in choking, coughing gasps. Beide him, King panted.

"If we can get to water, we'll be okay," Ricky mumbled.

King began to yelp and whine and snarl. Ricky knew that the dog was terrified by the fire smells brought to him on this sudden, strong wind. Ricky tried to move faster and couldn't. He couldn't seem to clear his lungs to breathe.

"What can you see, King?" he whimpered. "What's going on? Where are we?" Oh, God, if he could only tell where they were . . .

He could hear sounds, now—puffs and pops and snaps that chilled his blood. He recognized the sounds a fire would make—the crackling sounds, the roaring sounds. The geyser of noise recalled open fireplaces in winter, great bonfires at Boy Scout camp. A wave of acrid smoke made him choke.

Half sobbing, he crawled forward, then screamed with pain. Something sharp and barbed had pierced the palm of his left hand. He rolled over and over, sucking at his hand, wringing it. It hurt so badly that sweat poured down over his face and dripped into his eyes.

"That's it, that's it. I can't go on anymore!" What was the use? The pain throbbing in his hand intensified, and through the pain he shouted, "Get out of here, King! Get away! I'll only drag you down and get you killed, too!"

The dog yelped. Ricky could hear him bounding away, then returning. King wanted him to follow. Ricky shook his head. No way could he move any more—no way! He didn't know why he had tried to come all this way, anyway. It was useless!

"Get away!" he shouted and scrabbled weakly for some pebbles, which he threw at King. "You've got eyes, damn it! Get away from me and save yourself before this fire gets you, too!"

The dog barked loudly, and then Ricky felt the big beast come near. He felt sharp teeth nip down into his T-shirt, his shoulder. King started to tug

Ricky along, then stopped, panting. The big dog's strength, too, was ebbing.

He'll die because he won't leave me, Ricky thought miserably. He'll die because I'm so damned helpless!

Rage at his own impotence made him yell and bang his hands down on the ground. Then he shouted in hurt. He had forgotten that wounded palm. He sucked at the hurt again, then realized that whatever had wounded him was still embedded in his flesh. He plucked it loose, tearing more skin, bringing blood. It was a barbed fishhook, carelessly thrown away . . .

A fishhook!

"We're near the lake!" Ricky gasped. The thought made him reach into himself for one last ounce of strength, forced him to crawl forward. King barked and whimpered beside him. Ricky had no way of knowing where he was going. He trusted in King. King could *see* the water when they came to it.

The loudest boom Ricky had heard yet startled him into creeping faster. He realized that the fire was closer than he had thought. He had to hurry. Hurry . . .

His tired mind fled back in time to a day when he and Leo had run a race together. How long ago had that been? Ricky couldn't remember, but he could remember the fatigue and the pain, the light-headedness he had felt, and the dusty taste of thirst and exhaustion.

"One more foot forward," he muttered out loud. "Just one more step." He forgot that it was King and not Leo who paced beside him. "This is one crazy race, Leo. I don't think I'll ever finish it, man. Can you hear the people yelling and shouting? They're so noisy!"

The fire was so noisy . . . and it was getting hot. Hot and smoky. He would never finish this race. Never finish . . .

Ricky's fingers touched cool sand. Lake sand! He kept on going. His fingers touched water. They had reached the lake!

Ricky sobbed out loud as he plunged forward, flung his entire body into the lake. He was crying and laughing and he felt a little crazy, but the feeling was the most wonderful he had ever had in his life. He threw his body back into the water, and drank, and wept, and cried, "We did it! We made it!"

King started to bark again.

The barking steadied Ricky. Reality came crowding back into his mind. King was standing in the water near him, sniffing him, licking his face.

"I'm okay," he whispered, and put his arm around the short-furred body. "I'm okay, buddy. Mostly thanks to you."

But King was still worried. Why? Ricky wondered. They were in the water. Water could not burn. They had only to stay in the water, wait out the fire.

"What's wrong with you now?" he asked, as King yelped and whined. Was it that King was just afraid of the fire? Or was something else wrong?

Ricky forced himself to listen intently. He heard the roaring of the fire, the booming of falling trees. Then a blast of fire wind nearly knocked him senseless. The blast of wind was strong . . . *very* strong . . . and it was hotter than before. The fire had to be close to him, and it had to be burning fiercely.

Suddenly he could visualize what was happening, could see, in his mind's eye, the tongues of flame licking at dry fern, dry brier and brush, and then leaping into the branches of trees.

He could see the fire soaring to the tops of the tall trees, consuming them.

And if those roaring masses of flame fell into the lake, there would be no escape for anything in their path!

"We've got to go farther into the water, boy," Ricky said, trying to think, trying to keep his voice calm. He put his hand on King's shoulder, urging the animal forward. As they splashed farther into the lake, Ricky sensed that they were completely ringed by fire!

13

"Bobcat Lake is completely surrounded by fire!"

The helicopter pilot made his report over the chopper radio as he and his partner swung around the new perimeter of the Sector F fire. It was twelve thirty in the afternoon, and the noonday sun was nearly unbearable. Beneath them, the dark, even forest terrain was plumed with smoke.

An hour ago they had been ordered to leave another sector and head out to Sector F. They were supposed to hover over Bobcat Lake, scoop up lake water with the specially devised scoop attached to the copter, and then dump water over the heart of the raging fire.

But it wasn't possible. "We can't do it, Jake," the pilot said into his radio. "The fire's splintered off into several directions, and it's making an ungodly wind. Joe agrees with me that if we try to get down to lake level, the air currents might tear our chopper apart. If the wind shifts or dies, we can try a descent. Do you want us to stay out here and wait?"

The radio was silent. The pilot knew that Jake Simon was thinking hard. There were several other places where a copter could be used. All available aircraft had been called into action because of the fire, and every one was desperately needed.

"Fly low over the area one more time," Jake said finally. "The Talese boy is still missing. Swing as low as you can and see if there's any sign of him. Use your loudspeakers, too. Then, check back with me."

"Will do," The pilot rose over the burning lake and hovered away, helicopter motor unheard above the roar of the conflagration below. As the pilot headed toward the ruins of the Gallagher cabin, his partner scanned the terrain below.

"Any sign of the kid?" the pilot asked, after some time. "I don't like it, Joe. A blind kid wouldn't have gone too far. The search parties should have found him—*if* he was still okay."

"He had a dog with him, didn't he?" the man called Joe replied. "A police dog, they told me. Police dogs are terrific. They've got a fantastic way of protecting their owners. There could be a chance . . ."

"Even so, a helpless kid out in the forest for over twenty-four hours! Where's he going to get food and drink? He may have fallen and hurt himself— even knocked himself out. Then, there's the fire." The pilot shook his head. "I hope I'm wrong, but this could be a wasted trip."

His partner began to shout into the loudspeaker, "Ricky Talese, Ricky Talese, if you can hear us calling, make some sign. Ricky Talese, Ricky Talese, can you hear us?"

The chopper swung over the ruined cabin, around the woods on the other side. It was like looking for a needle in a haystack, looking for one lost boy and one lost dog in the forest!

"Ricky Talese, Ricky Talese, can you hear us? If you can hear us, make some sign. Ricky Talese, Ricky Talese . . ."

"There used to be a boat around here somewhere," Ricky told King as they waded deeper into the water. He slipped on the pebbles and soft silt underwater, recovered by steadying himself on King's shoulder. "I wish to heck I knew where that boat was! We could paddle out and stay in the center of the lake for a long time."

But probably the boat was burned by now! Ricky had no way of knowing which side of the lake they were on, but a fire like this would spread quickly.

King growled, deep in his throat, and Ricky felt something sinuous and swift brush by him. A fish, or . . . maybe a snake? Ricky knew that in a forest fire, all creatures took refuge in whatever water was available. He was sure that all around him were squirrels and fishers in temporary truce, shy bobcats, porcupines, foxes, terrified rabbits, and nervous deer.

"Is it coming closer, boy?" Ricky asked. "We'd better go farther in."

As he spoke, the wind brought billows of smoke across the surface of the lake. Ricky coughed, choked, and felt the blistering heat of the fire on the wind. Another gust made him gasp, cling to King. The lake was no place of safety. They could stew here as easily as they could burn on shore!

If only I could see, he thought. If only the accident had never happened. Leo would be alive, then, and King would be safe with the Gallaghers. A fierce pain rose in him, not just for himself and Leo, but for King. King deserved to make it. The dog had suffered so much, already, and he was brave and loyal.

"Too loyal," Ricky sighed. "You should've left me, King. You should've gotten out while you had the chance. Now it's too late."

King licked Ricky's cheek.

Another blast of hot air roared out at them. Ricky drew a deep breath and plunged underwater, taking King with him. The dog kicked and struggled, but when they surfaced the fire wind wasn't so intense.

Okay, Ricky thought grimly, we can duck under the water. But for how long can we keep it up? He remembered again those giant trees by the water's edge. He knew that they had better move farther into the lake before those trees burned and crashed into the water.

Wind roared again, and Ricky cried out in pain. Borne on the wind were hissing, smoldering bits of branch and the cinders of pinecones. One of the cones hit him on the shoulder and then fell, hissing and burning, into the water. Ricky submerged again, and this time he swam. When he resurfaced, he was neck-deep in water.

There was a splashing nearby and a wet, furry body butted against his side. King was swimming for his life! And King couldn't reach bottom here. Ricky pulled the dog close to him, thankful that King's heavy body was buoyant in the water. No way could he have hoped to "carry" King, otherwise!

Half supporting King, he waited for the next blast. It brought more smoke, more sizzling embers.

"If we stay out here, we'll fry or cook or bake," Ricky muttered. "We've got to go out even farther. But if we go too far, we'll drown. I can't swim for too long—not in the shape I'm in. And you can't either, King."

King moved against the boy, anchoring himself against Ricky's body. Ricky slid one arm around the big beast, helping King stay afloat. Then fire wind blasted again, and with the wind, this time, there came an ominous creaking sound that Ricky could hear above the roaring fire.

"King! Down!" he yelled, and dived, pulling the

dog with him. He swam as fast as he could to get away from what he knew was coming. Even so, underwater he felt the shock waves of something huge and heavy plunging into the water. Fear made him swim even harder, driving his exhausted body. When he surfaced, gasping and choking and coughing, the water felt warm. He tried to stand up and couldn't.

I'm way over my head, Ricky thought.

He turned, wanting to swim back to shallower water, and banged into something prickly. He backed off, then extended his hand curiously. It was a branch . . . and it wasn't burning. At least, it wasn't burning *now*. It had probably belonged to the huge tree that had crashed into the water. It must have been torn loose by the shock of the impact. Ricky tugged at the branch, felt it move sluggishly toward him. It was a big branch. A heavy, solid big branch.

King splashed near him. The dog was panting loudly, and there was a gasping quality in the panting that frightened Ricky. He's exhausted, Ricky thought. An idea came to him as the branch prickled against his side.

"I'm going to try and get you up onto this branch King. I don't know if it'll hold you, but it's worth a try. There isn't any other way."

He investigated the branch with his hands. It had a main stem, very thick and heavy, and many smaller branchlets that formed a kind of rude nest. Experimenting, he hauled himself up onto the branch. It rocked and slid around in the water, but even in the hellish wind, it didn't tip over. It was solid.

He whistled King over. The dog didn't understand, at first . . . and then, he didn't like the idea! Ricky grabbed the dog by the forepaws. King growled halfheartedly, but Ricky paid no attention.

"You've got to help me," he panted. "It's the only way to keep you from drowning. Up . . . you . . . go!"

He pushed King's forepaws onto the main branch, pushed and cajoled and coaxed the big dog up and out of the water. He held his breath and prayed as the branch swished and swayed and tilted, but it didn't turn over. Clinging to the branch with one hand, he reached out tentatively with the other. King was crouched in the "nest" made by the smaller branches.

King was all right! Ricky sighed deeply. Now, all they had to do was wait out the fire, somehow.

"It's going to be okay," he told King. "Don't worry, it'll be fine."

A blast of fire wind and smoke made him gag in the middle of his words. Who was he trying to kid? How could they be all right . . . in this? Ricky sensed that the fire wasn't burning itself out, but was spreading, encircling the lake. The fire would burn and burn, toppling great trees into the lake, sizzling the two of them with fire wind and choking them with smoke. And the heat . . . He could feel the heat now, reaching out to them across the water.

"We've got to move in deeper," Ricky told King.

He didn't dare let go of the branch, lest he lose King. He didn't climb onto it himself for fear of overbalancing it, but clung to it as he began to paddle with his feet. If only he knew which way to paddle! He didn't know whether he was going toward the fire or away from it. For all he knew, he could be heading right for shore, right for the fire.

"I'll paddle with the wind," Ricky murmured. "Fire must be blowing wind *out* at us, not sucking it in."

But that, he knew, could be wrong, too. He had heard that fires made their own winds, heard that they were unpredictable. A fire wind could shift, change direction.

King whined.

"It's your fault you're here," Ricky said. "You shouldn't have come with me. You should have made a break for it!"

But he knew why King hadn't gone. He reached out, fumbled for King's soaking body, patted the fur clumsily. Once, he had thought animals didn't have memories, but he would bet King did. Maybe King was remembering his long-dead owner. Maybe he was remembering things like kindness and loyalty and love.

"It's not fair," Ricky whispered. "This shouldn't be happening to us, not now."

Ricky kicked them along for a while longer, until he felt too exhausted to move his legs. Around him, the fire wind belched and wailed, and the sounds of trees crashing down or falling into the water grew louder and more frequent.

"I can't do any more," Ricky panted. "I can't. It's not fair."

He rested his forehead on his hands, wondering if anything was really fair. The accident, for instance. He thought of Leo, of the car crashing, of the hospital, and finally of his own blindness. He thought of the pain he had felt for his friend and his anger at his own helplessness. He remembered the bitter despair with which he had lived all this long while.

"Until you came," he said to King. "It changed, then . . ."

He thought of the way King had helped him, how King had dragged him out of that hole and rescued him from the fisher and later from the smoke. He remembered the warm touch of King's tongue on his cheek.

"It's not fair," Ricky yearned. "I want us to live!" With that thought came agony. It hurt a thousand times more than his old, lonely despair. Back then, he hadn't cared whether he lived or died. In fact, he had wanted to die! Wanting to live hurt a lot more.

Fire wind came again, and with it a blast of such foul smoke that Ricky nearly blacked out. His hands slackened on the branch, and he actually slid under the water. Then he resurfaced, shaking his head to clear it, determined to hang on.

"King!" he croaked. There was no answer except low panting from the dog. "Don't give up on me, old buddy! We'll make it, somehow. They've got to know this fire is happening. They'll be looking for us. They'll . . ."

Ricky stopped talking. Had he heard, above the roaring wind sounds, a different noise? A growling, stuttering sound?

"Helicopter!" he gasped. He was afraid to say the word out loud, even more afraid that he was mistaken. The sputtering, throbbing sound came closer.

"A copter! It's a copter! King, they're looking for us!"

Adrenalin raced through him, making him forget pain and weakness.

"They've found us! They've found us!" he screamed. "They'll get us out of here. Eeee-yowwwwww!"

King barked once, weakly.

Ricky let go of the tree branch, began to wave his hands frantically.

"Here we are! Here we are!" he yelled. "Here we are . . ."

There was a blast of wind that choked him, made

him duck under the water for relief. When he came up, the chopping sounds seemed to have disappeared.

"Don't go! No! Please don't go!" he shrieked.

Then, miraculously, he heard his own name being called. "Ricky Talese! . . . Ricky Talese! If you hear us, make some kind of sign!"

It sounded like God's voice, coming out of the darkness and through the fury of the fire. Ricky waved his arms again.

"Here I am! Here we are! Here . . ."

Wind, coming from a completely different angle, buffeted boy and dog and branch, causing the branch to rock and spin. King yelped in a panic of fear as Ricky felt the branch nearly overturn. He clung to the pitching branch, trying desperately to keep it steady and afloat. The voice from above spoke again.

"I see you, Ricky!"

It was a shout of triumph. Ricky felt ready to pass out with relief. But the relief was short-lived. The winds, which had been fierce up till now, worsened. Spinning and gagging, Ricky felt lungs and nostrils fill with smoke. There was an even harder gust of wind, and a loud splash indicated that King had fallen into the water.

"King!"

The dog was beside him, paddling desperately. What was that helicopter waiting for, anyway?

"Ricky!" The voice seemed to come from an even

greater distance now. "Listen to me, Ricky! We can't come down to get you. Do you understand? We don't dare come down there. The wind currents are very bad. You've got to hang in there, Ricky!"

The sound of the copter engine was faint above the roaring of fire and wind. Ricky had never experienced such winds! It was as if a tornado was funneling around him. His face and hands were singed, and he felt his hair frizz up and burn. Dust and ashes filled his nose, mouth, and ears. The keening, screaming, and shrieking wind surrounded him, but he could still hear King's panting bark beside him.

King couldn't stay afloat much longer. Neither can I, Ricky thought grimly. He was being tossed around like a cork. Desperately he grabbed for the branch and hung on.

"Stay with me, King, stay with me! We've got to make it," he cried. "We'll make it together, and Mom and Dad will adopt you and take care of you. After what you've done for me, they'll spoil you silly. You're a hero! You'll have steaks and bones and you'll get so fat you won't be able to move."

King's huge bulk crushed against Ricky. Instinctively Ricky let go of the branch with one hand and pulled the dog against him. None too soon, for the dog seemed spent. King lay panting against Ricky, unable to paddle or move. Ricky tried to turn the branch around so that King could creep up onto it again, but the wind came back, practically ripping the branch out of Ricky's weakened grasp.

Clinging to the branch, Ricky kept on talking. His words came in desperate gasps.

"Mom won't know what to do with you, at first. She likes little, cute dogs, and man, you are not a cute dog! But she'll have to get used to you. We're a team, dog. Hey, maybe you can be my seeing-eye dog. You've been my eyes all this time. Funny, I thought you might be a seeing-eye dog even before I met you."

Who was that chuckling and laughing and gasping out words? Dimly Ricky realized that it was he doing all these things.

How long? he wondered. How long can I hold on?

"I know the Gallaghers won't mind you coming home with me," he whispered. "We're going to make it together, dog."

"Ricky Talese! Ricky!"

The voice from the helicopter sounded faint above the noise around him. Ricky jerked his face upward.

"Ricky, this isn't any good. There are banks of smoke rolling out across the lake." Ricky lost a few sentences, and then he heard the man shout. "We daren't wait for the wind to drop. We're going to come down now, as best as we can and as close as we can. Then we'll direct you to swim toward us. Do you understand?"

He understood. There would be danger to the helicopter, coming down into this murderous wind, but they were coming!

"They're coming for us!" he sobbed. King stirred, moved by the sound of the boy's voice.

"Ricky! Listen to me, Ricky!" The unseen voice was urgent. "We can only come down one time, and we don't know how long we can stay down there. We can only take *you* out. I know you have a dog down there, but we can't take him, too."

Ricky couldn't believe what he was hearing. The man was saying that he'd have to leave King. How could he leave King?

"No!" he screamed, though his voice was instantly crushed in the wind. "I won't do it!"

"There's no other way.... We can't bring the dog up! If the wind wasn't so bad ... if he struggles, the whole chopper might go down! There's no time, and we can't risk it."

"No!" Ricky panted. "No-o-o-o!"

Wind gripped him, whirled him around, made him sob with pain and despair. The man was right. He knew that the man was right. How could they possibly rescue a heavy, struggling dog in this wind? Even if King didn't struggle, how could the helicopter linger long enough to haul King and then Ricky up to safety?

"You've got to think of yourself!" the voice was shouting. "We're coming down in a few seconds. The fire is burning very close to the water's edge. Once the smoke comes in, you'll suffocate."

Ricky felt numb. "I can't leave you," he sobbed to King. He could smell the smoke intensify, and he coughed and felt tears of pain and despair roll down his cheeks.

"Ricky, when you hear me yell 'Now!' let go of that branch and swim. I'll direct you. Do you understand, Ricky?"

The wind roared again, spewing more smoke.

"I can't leave you," Ricky whispered. The dog was sagging against him. Was King unconscious?

In his heart, he knew what had to be done. He knew that he had to leave King or be trapped here by the smoke and by the fire.

The wind roared once more, and Ricky gagged on the smoke. Then suddenly, without warning, the winds eased.

"*Now,* Ricky!"

14

Ricky let go of the branch. He let go of King. The dog made no sound. Was he dead already? Ricky prayed desperately that the big dog was dead, suffocated by smoke, no longer suffering. He prayed that King wasn't watching him swim toward the voice and the helicopter.

"Ricky, ... swim to your left. That's it! Good boy! Now, come straight ahead. Straight ahead, Ricky. ... That's great! We're only a few yards from you."

Now he could hear the whirring and chopping noises clearly above the fire sound. He swam toward the guiding noises, ignoring the tears that streamed down his face, pushing away the words that crowded his mind: "Good-by, King. Good-by, dog. I have to do this, don't you see? I'm sorry, but I have to do this. I didn't want to leave you, King, but there's no other way!"

The dog wanted him to live. King had saved him over and over again and would want him to survive. And he wanted to live, too.

"But I didn't want to live just for me," he whimpered. He had wanted King to make it, too. No ... push that thought away, Ricky, don't think about it! King was half dead, or maybe he was already dead. Desperately Ricky swam toward the guiding voice.

"Come on, Rick. You're almost there." The unseen voice was closer, urgent with hurry. Winds had picked up again, and they tore at Ricky as he swam. The air was full of smoke.

"Come on, Ricky. Hurry!"

He dived under the water, swam doggedly, pushing himself past all endurance. When he surfaced, he could hear the voice say: "Come on, Ricky. ... Here's the rope. It's coming down!"

There was a splash near him. He reached for the rope, but before he could grasp it, the wind came and tore it out of his hands. Choking smoke made him go underwater again, but when he resurfaced, the wind and the smoke were all around him.

"The rope! Get the rope. ... It's within a foot of you!"

Frantically he searched for it ... lost it again ... and finally seized it.

"Got it!" he croaked.

"Good boy. Now, feel the end. There's a loop, a kind of harness. Get your shoulders through it. Get it under your arms!"

Wind was tearing the rope from him again, but he hung on desperately, fumbled till he had the belt-like loop over his head. As he wrestled it over his shoulders, something heavy butted against his side. For a second, he felt panic . . . and then he realized what it was.

"King!" Ricky gasped.

The dog had followed him with his last strength. Ricky knew that King hadn't come with any hope of personal safety. He had come because he thought Ricky was in trouble again and needed him. King had come to help.

"Oh, King . . ."

Ricky forgot the rope, the helicopter, and even the fire. He put his arms around the big, exhausted beast, nearly drowning both of them.

"Ricky! Get into that harness!"

He had no choice. Ricky pulled the loop harness over his arms and shoulders, then stopped. No, he had no choice, so why did he have this bitter, empty feeling inside him? It was the same feeling that had been with him since the crash, since Leo's death and his own blindness.

Why should he feel this way now? He was going to live, wasn't he? He had struggled so hard to survive.

No, he thought. I didn't do anything. I couldn't have done anything alone! He remembered the dream, the one of the blind man sitting on his bed, forever staring into dark desolation.

"Now, Ricky . . . Hurry! Time's running out on us!"

The urgent shout from above made up his mind.

"I'm taking you with me," he told King. If he left King there, he would leave a part of himself. He would be like that blind man, lost and alone in the dark.

He pushed the rope harness lower, so that it fit around his waist, then he pulled King to him and positioned the dog crossways across his body. He wrapped one arm tightly around King, grasping the dog's body under the foreleg. Ricky wished for something to secure King to himself, but there was nothing. There was King's leash, but he didn't have the time to struggle with it.

"I'm ready!" he yelled, and prayed that he had the strength to hang on to King when they were both out of the water. "I'm ready! Pull us up!"

"You can't do it, Ricky! The dog will struggle. He'll pull us under."

"I'm not going without him!"

Ricky's scream was cut short by a blast of wind. He lay back against his loop harness and clung to King. King, he thought, if you struggle, if you do anything, I won't be able to hang on to you. I don't have the strength. You've got to trust me. We've got to do this together.

He rubbed his face against the coarse, wet hair of the animal's head, felt the flick of King's tongue against his face.

Slowly . . . slowly . . . the rope began to crawl upward. King began to thrash in panic.

"King, no!" Ricky forced calm authority into his voice. "Stay, King! Steady, big dog."

His arms were going to break off. He knew they were going to break off! Yes, and his chest was going to cave in from the weight of King struggling against him. Terrified, King lurched and scrambled to escape. Ricky felt the loop harness tighten vise-like around his back.

I'll never make it! I'll never manage to hold on! he thought.

"King," he whispered, "please . . . please!"

Inch by inch they were being drawn up toward the copter. Now the chopper itself was climbing, bearing them out of the water. Now, they dangled in smoke-thick air.

How could he keep hold of King? He couldn't even breathe! Ricky felt his senses slipping away, fought grimly to stay conscious. He couldn't black out . . . not now! If he did, he'd lose his hold on King.

"Good boy, King. Easy, boy. Easy . . ."

King's struggles lessened.

Above, the voice sounded nearer. "We'll have you up here in a minute, Ricky. Hang on, now!"

"Hang on," Ricky told himself. "I've got to hang on." He gritted his teeth against the ash and wind and pain, and clung to the dog.

And then, they were being hauled up, and there were hands on Ricky's shoulders, and they were tumbling into a heap on the chopper floor. The helicopter rocked and spun in the wind, and then began its crooked, crablike ascent.

The man who had pulled them up was leaning over Ricky, asking questions. Ricky couldn't make sense of the words.

"Take care of my dog," he whispered. "Is King all right?"

He heard a voice say clearly: "Your dog will be all right. He's in tough shape, but he'll be fine, thanks to you." Ricky could hear King panting next to him.

"King," he murmured. He felt the reassuring, warm touch of the dog's tongue on his cheek.

Another voice now spoke.

"It's a miracle, that's what it is, you surviving that holocaust! We're heading back toward Fire Headquarters now, son. Your friends and parents are waiting there." There was a pause. "How do you feel?"

Ricky ached all over. His face was burned raw, his hair all singed off, and it hurt to breathe.

He felt wonderful!

He locked a tired, aching, triumphant arm around King and drew the big dog close. I held on, he thought. We made it, King, you and me! We made it together.

About the Author

Maureen Crane Wartski teaches high school English in Sharon, Massachusetts. Born in Japan, she has lived in Bangkok with her husband and two boys, all now U.S. citizens. She writes stories and books for adults as well as young people. Her books MY BROTHER IS SPECIAL, A BOAT TO NOWHERE, and A LONG WAY FROM HOME are also available from Signet Vista.